The Life I Owe Her

Allison Meldrum

To my children, William and James, who are my greatest source of inspiration and joy.

Prologue

Edinburgh Royal Infirmary, 2000

It's a choice, Ava told herself. A choice, just like any other in life. Once it was made, she could move on and live beyond this moment; live in a world where all that would be in her past.

Except it wasn't an easy decision to make. She wasn't picking a colour to paint her living room or whether to pay for her car over two years or five. Within the hour, she had to choose which one of her newborn babies she would give away forever.

"Your visitor's here, love. You decent?"

The midwife spoke in the monotonous tone of someone who couldn't understand what that moment meant. She shuffled, probably waiting for Ava to acknowledge her presence.

"Strange business, this one, that's for sure."

Don't you dare judge me, you old cow. You know nothing about me.

Even the briefest look into the eyes of her children hypnotised Ava, and love — inescapable, all-encompassing love — seemed to envelop her. Losing herself in their tiny faces, satin skin, and intoxicating smell, she wondered how she had managed to give birth to something so perfect. Delivered into a world that was rolled in the glitter of a new millennium but had woken to a hangover of chaos and uncertainty.

As she compared their differences, Ava couldn't decide which one she needed more or which one she loved more; she *had* to, however. Right now.

Tramadol and codeine bore down on her mind, and she forced herself to focus on her visitor and what their presence meant. One of her babies was about to be taken from her arms and given to someone else. The smell of their comfort would not be the same. Their skin would feel alien. Their voice wouldn't be the one heard from inside the womb. That was the deal, and there was no way out.

Choose now, Ava. This is your only option.

Shifting with painful determination, she reached for the baby carrier that the midwife had nestled beside her bed and laid both girls down. While she tried to wrap a blanket around them, something contracted in her belly.

How can you be so different already?

She knew they would not be identical, but she still didn't expect this. One had a full crown of silken, chocolate-brown hair, and the other had deep-set eyes and more delicate features. The way they moved, too — one wriggling, as if she was responding to the midwives' radio, while the other drifted towards sleep. Ava imagined thousands of other millennium babies being welcomed by parents who already had their future planned out for them.

Staring at her second twin, born three minutes after the first, Ava noticed that she was curled up on herself, shying away from a world that looked bright and intimidating. Her head was angled to Ava. The need she felt coming from that child made her reach out and touch her delicate cheeks.

Would this be the last time I touched you? Or will it be you I see grow up beside me?

At once, the room felt too hot. Visiting hours were starting, and Ava became aware of the sound of footsteps filling the corridor. It was the sound of excitement and expectations, of flower bouquets crinkling and bouncing off helium balloons. It all fired straight into Ava's head. She wanted to disappear under the starched white covers of her hospital bed.

Closing her eyes to block reality out didn't help, however. The voice she was dreading to hear cut through the drone. It had a soft tone with a hint of an accent.

"Room eight, first bed on the right, doll," the ward sister said. She had an air of authority about her. "I'll be along shortly. Plenty to sign with this business."

As the door opened, sickness rose in Ava's stomach. She knew the next few moments were all about survival, and she gathered the strength to sit up and face her visitor.

Said visitor, a woman, was expensively dressed. The designer labels weren't visible, but Ava knew they were hiding behind fur collars and cashmere. Even her perfume smelt pretentious. She was trying to make eye contact with Ava first, rather than look at the babies lying in the hospital cot that divided them. Ava would not meet her gaze, however, and she allowed herself to take her first proper look at the newborns.

"They're so perfect. So—"

"They're too hot. It's... this room is..." Ava looked down at her bedsheets. She needed this to be over, and soon. "You need to choose. I can't. I just can't.

"How are you feeling?"

Don't. Don't go there.

"I mean it. Make the choice yourself."

Looking once more at her angels, Ava knew she had to pay her debt. *It's the only way to be free from it all. From him.* And yet, tears and exhaustion were about to overwhelm her. *Practicalities*, she thought. She had to find shelter in practicalities.

"They know. This lot knows what's happening," Ava said, pointing to the midwives. She could feel their stares, but they didn't dare to make eye contact. "I've already signed everything they need."

"Take your time, Ava. It's a tough day. I get that."

"Did you bring the car seat?"

Both women were shirking the hardest of choices now.

"Let's make this decision together?" the woman said in the end.

Again, Ava looked down. The babies were snuggled together, just as she had imagined them when she first felt the flutters. Then the kicks, the unrelenting kicks, and the dancing on her bladder, a constant reminder of their growing presence. Even though she was told they were not 'identical', she couldn't escape the image of two entwined beings. Interconnected, like the yin and yang symbol. Seeing them like that just emphasized their size difference.

"Were you the womb bully then, young lady?"

The baby's body was longer and broader, and her tiny fingers looked chunkier than her sister's and more ready to grasp the world.

"I don't think I can…"

No. Don't expect me to take the pain away for both of us here.

"You must, and we all walk away with no regrets. Stick to the plan, okay?"

Shrieks, laughter, and an argument over who would get the first cuddle erupted from a nearby cubicle. Ava felt sick and tried to focus on something else. A piece of shiny equipment; the window; anything at all to anchor herself. All too soon, though, her attention shifted to her babies. Their eyes were closed. The world was still too much for them to take in.

I don't blame you. Close those precious eyes, my angels.

"I think this little one may be stronger willed," Ava said, pointing to the slightly larger bundle that lay between them.

"Do you? How can you tell?"

"Maybe she'll adjust better to being without her sister —" Ava watched the woman's arm stretch out and wanted to tear it away from her body. Right there, in front of everyone. She kept talking. "—but this one, she's sleeping soundly. She won't know until she wakes. That's easier, right?

"I can give you some more—"

"No, time won't help. Time won't make this hurt any less. Said I'd decide when they were born, and that's what I'm going to do. I told myself I'd keep the child who seemed to... heck, I don't know... need me more."

Ava knew today should be the happiest day of her life, but she couldn't breathe. How could she ever look back and feel good? The memories would torture her forever. It needed to be over soon. She placed her hand on the forehead of the child whose eyes were wide open, then she embraced her with care, as if she was made of porcelain.

The woman reached out again, maybe sensing that it was the right moment. Ava clung to each wriggle one last time before adjusting the soft blankets around her.

"Take her right now. Hold her tight. Please."

As she handed over the baby, Ava could see the feeling of completeness that washed over the woman. She enjoyed an unexpected and fleeting moment of calm before the gut-wrenching sadness returned, fuelled by the sound of the baby's cries.

It was too much to bear.

Turning her back, she tried to block them out as they left the room. There would be no goodbyes. Not today. They had agreed on a plan and they were going to stick to it. She had no choice but to focus on what was left of her world.

Her debt had been paid. Now, she just had to live her life as a single mother of only one daughter.

Chapter 1

AVA

Edinburgh, 2006

Ava Peterson was a woman on the edge most days of the week. A situation not helped by the thought that everything she owned was on its last legs, not least her car. The boot of her ageing red Vauxhall Astra refused to close again. A trick it kept pulling on her when it was least welcome. Today, however, for the sake of her six-year-old, she would stay in control and avoid the *bat-shit crazy mother* territory.
Hold it together, she thought, forcing her full body weight against the filthy, scratched nemesis.

Ava could still turn heads. Five feet and seven inches tall, and almost in her thirties, she still had her thick, caramel blond hair still looked magnificent, even if now it was getting sweaty around her face. She had maintained an enviable figure all her adult life, largely due to being a constant hive of activity. Her skin had a translucent quality that meant she needed little makeup other than a lick of mascara and lip gloss(to face the world).

Determined to fix the boot with sheer brute force alone, she gave it another shove with her hip.

"Christ! Not again. Throw me a fecking bone, world, please!"

An overdue payment had brought her bank account back from the dead, and she'd treated herself to two bottles of Tesco's finest Cabernet Sauvignon. There were too many hours standing between her and that delicious cork-popping moment that defined a Friday evening, though. Opening the boot again, and trying to rearrange the contents, she dumped her groceries on top of a muddy bike, some wellies, and an old microwave oven. The oven had been in her car since a failed gum tree sale, and it would remain there for now, awaiting its fate.

"Mummy, put the stuff on my knees."

"What's that, love? I got the blue Pringles, yes."

"No, mum. The shopping. My knees — here."

Catherine was only six, but she could already outsmart Ava in times of panic.

"Thanks, honey. Good plan."

After balancing some toilet rolls, a jumbo-sized box of Weetabix, and three overflowing shopping bags around Catherine's booster seat, Ava returned to the rear of her car to give it a final slam.

"Mum? Are we going to be late?"

"Late? Us? Not a chance, Catherine!"

Ava noticed her daughter's face in the rear-view mirror and felt a spontaneous giggle escape, releasing some of the tension. Catherine mirrored her action almost at once.

"Mummy, we're *always* late."

"Are we? Really?"

"*Every* time."

"Ah, we just like to make an entrance, don't we, my love?"

Catherine gave her a disapproving look. She'd already perfected it. Learned, Ava feared, from her.

Arriving at a pretty, three-storied terraced house in New Town, she saw pink balloons and bunting adorning the wrought-iron gate. It reminded her of a birthday card she had once received from some distant friend of her parents. Even then, she'd found it repulsive. All that glitter and unnecessary padding and gold trim. Just like the gate facing them, it felt fake and strangely intimidating. Ava sensed her daughter's nerves projecting towards her from the back seat.

"Mummy, I feel a bit sick-ey."

Switching off the engine and waiting for its sad spluttering to end, she turned around and looked her daughter straight in the eyes.

"Is it the sickness you feel when you've eaten too much ice cream?"

Catherine shifted in her seat, staring out of the window with her hand resting on her forehead, as if considering her answer.

"Or is it the sickness you feel at the start of a new school term?"

"It's the school sick, Mummy."

"Hm. Do you think it might go away when you taste the birthday cake?"

Her face filled with tension and Ava turned around to give her an encouraging smile.

"I don't know, Mum. I just don't."

"Why don't we go and investigate, then?"

As predicted, they were the last ones to arrive, and the party was in full swing already. Small groups had formed throughout the garden, like tightly shut Venus Flytraps. Ava watched as her daughter took in the scene, humming to herself and seeming to shrink in size. Every fibre of Ava's being wanted to turn around and take her to the park instead — to save her from navigating this hostile world of junior *mean girls*. And yet.

"Come on, honey. Let's show everyone that beautiful dress." Taking her hand, Ava walked her daughter up to the door, where she released Catherine into the arms of the hosts. The greetings she exchanged with the other parents were full of the over-the-top fakery she remembered from her childhood parties, packed with air-kissing, empty pleasantries, and mutual shows of wealth.

Catherine was pretending to be brave, so Ava rolled out her version of the relaxed mum, even if they were both rubbish at pretending.

"I'll be back soon, angel. I love you," she said, and she meant it. She meant every single word, because good mothers never let their children down. They were always there, where they were needed. Without question.

Ava's own mother, Mollie, had few interests in life. The first one was spending her husband's money; the second one was the strong gin and tonic she had at three pm, and the last one was herself. Her greatest love. There was little room for nurturing a child.

"Don't be late, Mum. Please."

"Pinkie promise, I won't."

Ava winked at her daughter in a show of further reassurance before turning to leave. The temptation to turn around for one last glance was strong, but Ava ignored it and began her (mental) calculations as soon as she made it to her car.

Two hours of party time, minus two-times fifteen in the car, it gives me ninety minutes of child-free time at home, she thought. *The world is my bloody oyster, for ninety precious, succulent minutes. Get that white paper done, sent, and slam on a washing load.*

Ava broke her days down like that, and there was little breathing room left for anything else. Completing tasks was hard enough as it was.

The constant loop in her mind screamed, *'what's next?'*, followed by, *'is it finished?'*, before moving on to, *'good enough? It'll have to be'*. Then, the odd, *'is it payday yet?'*, would rear its head, just to keep things interesting. And so it went on and on. She imagined her brain as an old-fashioned wooden toy: hammer down one shape and another one would pop right up, while an inescapable feeling of falling short, of not being good enough, gnawed at her.

As she pulled out onto the main road, Ava saw her husband's face flashing on her phone, accompanied by the ringtone he's linked to his calls. Sean thought that *Mr Brightside* was both ironic and hilarious; Ava found it irritating, but she had neither the time nor the nous to change it.

Not now, Sean. I have ninety minutes. They are all accounted for, and a conversation with you is not included.

Sean calling during the day was most likely related to practical or urgent matters, and she struggled to find the capacity for either. The lyrics faded out, but two minutes later, his face flashed up again as she approached a right turn. That sodding song again. His persistence was out of character, though. Stretching to find the hands-free cable, Ava felt the familiar texture of wrapping paper.

"Shit. I forgot to give her the present. Shit."

Ava's mind was flooding with images of a *judgemental party mum* pitying the child who arrived empty-handed.

Totally dysfunctional. I told you. Judgy party mum would be revelling in this ultimate social faux pas. She could hear the Morningside accent cutting through as she imagined her equally judgy husband standing next to her, nodding in agreement.

Morningside was one of the most exclusive neighbourhoods in Edinburgh. Many families who lived there were pleasant and hard-working people, but some of them were the very essence of city snobbery, with their inherited wealth, large cars, and private school obsessions. Ava hadn't taken the time to decipher which camp the birthday party people fell into, so she imagined the worst. Maybe they were just like her own mother, a possibility that turned her stomach.

While she looked for a safe place to turn around and head back to the party, a few words from the radio cut through her thoughts.

— Premier League Striker Ricky Petrie has been cleared of all wrongdoing in relation to charges of sexual assault. Speaking outside Edinburgh's High Court, top criminal defence lawyer Michael Miller said his client was relieved to clear his name and focus on serving the club he is devoted to professionally —

She reached out to turn up the volume, and when she glanced up, she caught the expression of a van driver who was coming from the opposite direction.

Oh, God.

There was less than a hair's breadth between the vehicles after she steered wildly around him, but he passed her by, and the blast of his horn shook Ava to the core. Her car came to a sudden crashing halt in the closest ditch, inches away from a solid brick wall.

Holy cow, Ava, you stupid, stupid idiot.

Minutes later, having moved her car to the relative safety of a lay-by, she looked down at her hands. They were still shaking against the wheel, which was wet with sweat. And yet, an overwhelming feeling of relief washed over her. She could have been crushed by that van. She could have hit that wall at full speed. It could have all been over. It was a feeling she'd had before. Back then, the first time she'd escaped death.

Someone's still got my back. Lucky sod.

Hoping for her breathing to return to normal, she stared out of the window and waited until the next news report broke through the music. She needed to know if she had heard it right the first time. She needed to know if he was back.

#

Ava struggled back from the sweet warmth of her dream, becoming aware of the grip around her hand. It was the perfect mix of strong and soothing. And, even through the dreamy haze, a smile that was full of mischief and passion in equal measure. She would do anything to keep that smile unchanged.

"Morning, sleepyhead."

Everything still felt out of focus.

"Have I slept in?"

"You needed it."

"What time is it? I told you to wake me."

"Settle down, it's Sunday. Day of rest, remember?"

"Not religious, Sean, remember?"

"Yup, you swear too much."

God, I love this man, she thought. There was no one she would rather see as she pulled herself back into the real world. Well, almost no one.

Mornings were often hard. A face often drifted into her mind, and she wondered what her other angel was doing and where she would be waking. How different was her life from theirs? It took Ava a few moments to focus on the real world — to responsibilities, logistics and overdue bills.

"Where's Catherine?"

"Downstairs, overdosing on some horrendous American tv. Why don't you just stay here? I'll take her out — once round the park or something?"

Everything urged her to get up and get on with life, but aching fatigue was gripping her whole body.

"Thanks, honey. I think I will close my eyes for a bit longer. Enjoy the park."

She succumbed to the warm embrace of her duvet within minutes.

"You were one stressed cookie last night," said Sean. "What was spinning in that head of yours?"

Memories of her near-miss with the van rushed in. The sound of that name over the airwaves. It had been six years since she last heard it.

He's back, and he won't be alone. I have to find a way to tell Sean.

"You don't want to know, honey. Trust me."

"Yep, that's probably true."

Shortly after Sean left, Ava curled back into the cocoon of her sheets, feeling intoxicated by the smell of her husband on the mattress and the escape from the day ahead. As she stretched her limbs, she caught sight of the scar across her right ankle. It was paler now, but a reminder of the day when her teenage self-sought adventure. Ava could still feel the tangle of weeds that held her underwater, and the memory caused her breathing to quicken and her skin to cool down, so much that she pulled up her duvet. Just like that, she was restless.

She turned on her side and pulled at the drawer of her bedside table, reaching for a photograph with a wooden frame, before staring into those hazel-brown eyes. The same eyes she saw when she got rescued from the water, and the arms that carried her to dry land were youthful like her own, but stronger than anyone could believe.

Her memories of that day were still so muddled. Even after closing her eyes, the face in the photo wouldn't disappear. It was a face she would never forget, no matter how much time had passed.

Chapter 2

SYLVIE

Glasgow, 2006

The neighbourhood of Bearsden had been Michael's choice. According to him, it was the only suitable part of Glasgow to relocate his family from rural France. Just a few miles from the centre of Scotland's largest city, it ranked second place in the *Sunday Times' Best Places to Live*. And not without cause. Sylvie listened in earnest as he read her the newspaper extract. *Bearsden is an affluent and leafy suburb of Glasgow. Housing a classic mix of Victorian villas, it offers a suburban village feel, among the best schools in the region, and an embarrassment of culinary riches. Hard to imagine a better place to raise a family.*

Michael told her it was the perfect fit for 'his' family of three. His own Scottish childhood had been one of cheap shoes, cheaper food, and humiliation. Now, having made legal partner at the age of twenty-eight, he was never seen out without a smart suit, plenty of hair gel, and smelling of something beguiling.

It astounded Sylvie that any man had shown her some attention. She always pretended not to notice that her best friend was the one who got it all. It was Ava who received the winks, the wolf whistles, and the date invitations. Sylvie hid in the background and felt awkward.

Staring at her reflection in the gold-framed mirror of the hallway, Sylvie noticed how the light caught her brown hair. She often wore it pulled up in a bun, just the way her mum did. It gave her a sense of comfort. A few strands had come loose in front of her ears and she tied them back in place: Michael liked it best like that, all neat and tidy. He liked most things neat and tidy, and besides, he could admire the curve of her neck better that way.

When they first moved to France six years ago, it wasn't part of the agreement but he convinced her that returning to her native country was the only way everything would work out back then, Sylvie stood by his choice. Just as she did when he decided it was time to return to Scotland. He knew what was best for them, and how to make it happen; he was a fixer, and they were lucky to have that in their lives. Sylvie had to remind her daughter of that when she got upset   , but it would build resilience. One day, she would understand   .

She watched as the delivery trucks loaded elegant furniture in through the entrance to their new home. The neighbours were probably watching on as elements of their French life made their appearance in this new world.

"It's just as perfect as I'd hoped for."

Michael's statement felt irrefutable as they looked at his computer screen. Images of the house in France stared back at them.

"We're going to be blissfully happy, aren't we?"

His questions had a rhetorical undertone, but Sylvie seldom disagreed. She was returning to the country where she'd learned to live without her parents, without the centre of her world. The country where life had broken her out of her sheltered childhood.

Shifting her way past the pile of boxes in the hallway, she knocked a few out of place, revealing the parquet flooring underneath. It was impactful. It would make a statement of style and class to any visitors as soon as they entered. She knew Michael would like that. Sylvie wandered upstairs to the master bedroom, feeling a little like the child playing hide and seek in a stranger's home. Somebody had already left a few labelled boxes there, and she reached for one, looking for something familiar to cling to. It was a box of journals, the only one she'd packed herself.

"Ah, thank God."

The words trickled quietly out of her lips as she lifted old leather-bound diaries and journals, opening them with care. Notes and photos fell from the pages, and each of them had a date scribbled on.

February 7th, 1989, School Leavers Day. July 16th, 1992, Second Year Arts Faculty Ball, she read.

An image of herself, younger and with her arms draped around a blond with a mischievous smile, popped up. As much as her heart longed to feel that embrace again and see that carefree smile again, Sylvie knew she had made a promise to her husband that would keep them apart.

He trusts me to stay away from them.

After tucking the photos back in, she put everything away, concealed with a linen scarf.

I haven't forgotten you, Ava. I promise.

Chapter 3

AVA

Edinburgh, 2006

Ava met Sean five days after Catherine's first birthday. The day was etched in her memory for the strangest of reasons. Edinburgh was going through a bone-numbing cold November morning, and all Ava wanted was a double espresso and some reliable Wi-Fi. Catherine was in her second week at the nursery, and she'd sidestepped the weepy mothers lamenting their anxiety separation as she left the building. She wasn't immune to these emotions either, but she didn't have time for them. She wore the badge of a single parent, which made her feel like an outsider, and indulging in such things wasn't going to pay the nursery fees. For the next five hours, she needed to be free and productive.

He was standing in front of her in the queue at Costa - a Double-shot Americano man flirting over his breakfast choice.

"Bacon roll or sausage roll, that is the question."

The pretty brunette serving him was doing a poor job of looking impressed.

"Sir? Can I help you, Sir?"

"What would you recommend?"

"Er, I'm vegan."

"Ah, right? Fair enough. I really must try that sometime."

Oh, Christ, could you do this another time? Some of us are on a deadline here.

"Ahem."

It was an unsubtle cough, but Ava didn't care, until he turned round and looked at her straight in the eyes. Double-shot Americano man had a smile that made her feel sixteen again. It lit up his entire face. That day, he left Costa with Ava's number.

At first, Sean's confidence infuriated her, and she hated how attracted she was to him. She didn't realise she had boxes to tick until he ticked every single one. The physical part ate at her self-restraint, too. His eyes, his olive skin, his body, muscled but in a subtle way, and how he never took his eyes off her when she talked.

I know how to make you run for the hills, Double-shot man, she thought.

"I have a daughter. Catherine; she's called Catherine."

"Okay."

"She's only a year old, and she still doesn't sleep through the night. That makes me a single parent, just so you know."

"Awesome."

Ava was astounded that his reaction showed no sign of concern for her baggage.

"What's wrong with you? Have you got no respect for your own freedom, you lunatic?"

"Apparently not." His next comment came with utter determination. "Oh, sorry. Were you expecting me to bugger off at the prospect of sharing your affection with a small human? Sorry to disappoint."

"Bloody hell. Where do you come from, anyway?"

His persistence paid off in the end and Sean became more interwoven with Ava's life with every passing month — much to her own frustration. His job as a self-employed photographer meant he couldn't offer much financial support. Still, he could bring an abundance of love and cooking skills. As a result, Catherine was raised in a home that was chaotic, warm, and never boring. Whether she admitted it or not, this was the starkest of comparisons with Ava's own memories. Childhood birthdays for Ava had been a rare occurrence. If something reminded her parents in time, a card with cash stuffed inside would appear, and she would spend on something inappropriate and meaningless, like a body piercing, just to annoy them.

"Looks like it'll be a while before you're trusted to make good financial decisions, young lady. Or any sensible decision." Her father's words were soul destroying, but easier to accept than question.

I will show you, with every fibre of my being, that you are so, so wrong.

Before she met Sean, Ava would start every month figuring out how much to spend on Catherine's needs, followed by the household bills. She had been the sole provider for her daughter, and being a freelance public affairs consultant meant her wage wasn't a fixed one. It was a tightrope of lonely decisions and gambles, but she had walked it.

Talk to me. Let me know how I can help.

Sean would try his best to carve out a role for himself, and Ava couldn't let him all the way in.

#

It was the first Sunday after her near accident that Ava was met with a sea of balloons, banners and cakes as she padded sleepily into the kitchen. The overall look reminded her of the unsold dregs at a summer fayre. But then, the panic set in. She would have to be knocked unconscious to have forgotten her own daughter's birthday, so it couldn't be that.

Shit. Is it Sean's? Or our anniversary?

Before she had a chance to think anymore, Catherine came bounding towards her, her face alight with joy.

"Sweetheart, I'm so so —"

"Happy birthday, M   ummy!"

She turned around. From the corner, Sean was giving her the thumbs up, and a wave of relief engulfed her.

"We love you *sooo* much!"

"Right, ah — thanks. Yes, my birthday! Of course!"

Sean mouthed *you forgot?*, and Ava nodded in his direction.

"Well, it looks like a tiger came to tea in here."

"Don't be silly, Mum!"

"Who's going to tidy all this up?"

Sean shot her a look. "Jeez, Ava, it's your birthday. Could you try and not be the grown-up for an hour or so, at least?"

"Sorry, did I say that out loud?" she answered. "This is lovely, thank you."

Every part of her wanted to relax and enjoy the moment, just like Sean suggested, but something was niggling her mind. It was the niggle of someone who knew how many bills they had to pay that month; the poking and prodding of the awareness that most months she was the greater breadwinner. That wasn't a problem, really. It was just a thing that niggled… and made her say tactless things.

"Very thoughtful of you both. Especially since Daddy has all that new work to get to grips with, too. How's the new client coming on, anyway? Anything interesting?"

The loaded compliment rebounded off her husband's thick skin.

"Nah, Ava, I turned it down."

"You did?"

"Yep. It wasn't good timing, and I thought you might just want me around a bit more?"

"To do what?"

"Well, you're always telling me how you don't have time to breathe, so I thought you could use some extra help at home —"

" — Catherine, don't put those cups there. They'll stain the wood —"

" — You know, help with Catherine, too?"

"Ava, why don't you just try to enjoy your birthday? Live in the moment a bit? There's a time and place for work."

The same resentments kept bubbling to the surface on hearing his words. Ava somehow found the strength to bite her tongue.

Ava noticed how Catherine was looking at them and hated herself for exposing their daughter to their verbal tussles. Catherine should exist in a world without any real-world problems for as long as possible.

"Anyway," Ava said, "I'm lucky! I have you both to play with at my birthday party!"

Let it go, not today.

"Right then," Sean said. "Who's for pizza and cake? Or cake on pizza?"

Catherine's face scrunched up and she let out a strange noise that cut off the tension.

Watching Catherine and Sean move around the place overwhelmed Ava little by little until fear poisoned her mind. *That van driver. He nearly hit you yesterday,* she thought, and the mere idea of what could have happened cut through her heart. *You almost lost everything.*

#

The day went by in a haze of cake-eating and the kind of non-productive nonsense that Ava hated the most.   She hated it for many reasons but, mostly, because it forced her to think. By the time evening came around, she was more exhausted than she could bear. She needed to be released from her own mind by the one person who could do that better than any. Sean. Her imperfect, but strong and comforting husband.

Ava waited in silence, hugging the cup of milky tea that Sean had made for her before taking Catherine up to bed. She felt an uncontrollable urge to rip off the metaphorical plaster right away. And as soon as he sat down next to her, she knew he had clocked the intensity in her eyes.

"Sean, I almost had a car accident yesterday."

"Pardon?"

"It was all my stupid fault."

"You what?"

"There was a van, and I almost hit it. When you were calling. Not that I'm trying to blame—I was trying to find the hands-free cable, and it just came out of nowhere."

"Ava, I've told you already, don't use the bloody thing when you're driving."

"I thought there was an emergency! You called me twice! What was it about, anyway? I nearly crashed into   a van, Sean. *Sean*."

"But, you didn't?"

"No, but…"

"And no one was hurt?"

Ava shook her head.

"You're just tired. Let it go."

"Catherine could have lost her mother."

"But she didn't. It's okay, and we need to get on with life."

Still, panic rose inside her; she couldn't let go. And something had released the floodgates of parental worry in her head. She had his attention and felt the need to delve further.

"Do you think she's happy?"

"What do you mean, Ava? Happy that you came home in one piece? I'm going to take a risky guess here, but I reckon the answer to that would be a firm yes."

"No, Sean. I mean, in general. Is she, you know… happy in general?"

She waited for him to reassure her like he always did. This time, though, he was silent. Something in his eyes scared her.

"What is it?"

"It's nothing."

"What?"

"No, listen. Now is a crap time. It's your birthday. You're full of pointless anxiety. Let's do this tomorrow."

"Christ, Sean, what is wrong with you?"

"What, aside from my wife having a manic episode and trying to take out a lorry?"

Ava ignored his sarcasm.   "What did you want to say?"

"It's probably nothing, but I found something in Catherine's room."

Again, panic rose, but it was a different kind of panic. It was dizzying and all-consuming. "Sean, you're scaring me. What is it?"

"She's been drawing."

Ava laughed. It sounded awkward. "Drawing?"

"No, I mean, she's been drawing loads. And, um, some of it's… it's disturbing stuff."

"Like what?"

Sean's face was losing its soft edges while he went to open one of the cabinets below the TV.

"I put some of them in here, so she wouldn't notice they're missing. I just believe this is a pretty accurate snapshot."

She put her cup down and reached for them. Trepidation made her want to put them straight into the bin, but she knew better.

It all stared back at her   in every drawing. Some featured a child standing on her own while other children were crowded together in the distance. Some showed her favourite TV characters looking sad and lonely too. The colours were dark and joyless, broken only by some red. Ava picked up a drawing of a girl with a tear falling from her eye, and it felt like her own.

"Oh God, Sean. I had no idea. She's in so much pain. She's trying to tell us…" Lost in her thoughts, Ava looked up to see the confusion on her husband's face.

"Pain? Telling us what? What do you think she's trying to say?"

Ava fell silent. That was it. She had to tell him. If Sylvie had returned to Scotland, she was going to find them, and Sean needed to know everything.

He's a good man. He loves me. He'll understand.

"Sit down, Sean. We need to talk."

Chapter 4

AVA

Edinburgh 2006

Ava woke up at dawn, with the early light blazing through the windows of her room. The street was full of young families, with cars that looked as overworked as their owners and mortgages that would make retirement a distant dream for decades. But it nudged at the edges of the catchment area for a great primary school, and she wanted to give Catherine the best shot at success that she could.

Her sleep had been unexpectedly peaceful. The night before, Ava had told Sean everything. She'd told him about the day she almost drowned. She'd told him how she was so drunk she lost two hours. She'd told him how she came to, lying on the riverbank with Sylvie watching over her. He just listened as Ava explained she wouldn't be here without Sylvie, that Catherine wouldn't exist, and that their family owed everything to this friend he'd never met.

"Where is she now, this Sylvie?"

"Give me a chance, Sean —"

" — You know, your life-saving soulmate. Why haven't I heard about her until now?"

"There's more. A lot more."

Sean's face paled, but Ava kept talking. He listened, and she could see how hard it was for him to keep silent as she explained the friendship that had saved her from two parents too detached to care about her.

he knew from his blank face that none of it made sense. He couldn't understand; no one could, unless they had the same kind of bonding.

"When she hurts, you feel it, too," she told him, tearing up as she lived through that pain once more. "When she laughs, you do, too, but harder and longer. There's nothing in the world the both of you wouldn't do for each other."

He nodded and looked lost.

"Where is this going?"

His voice sounded calm. To Ava, it felt as if she was speaking to a stranger.

"When Catherine was born, she… she, oh, God." *There's no going back now.* "She wasn't alone."

"What do you mean?"

"She was a twin, Sean."

Confusion was written all over his face. Confusion and devastation.

"Ava? What happened? Did they live?"

"Yes, Sean. Her twin didn't die. She was perfect. They both were."

He didn't reply and Ava ploughed on, her face lowered.

"She was born three minutes after Catherine. Beautiful and different in so many ways. Bigger, stronger—"

"And what happened to her?"

"I gave her to my best friend," she said, noting the growing anger in his voice. It cut into her heart. "I gave her to Sylvie."

He didn't speak again that day. Ava could only watch as her husband left the room. She heard him walk upstairs and recognised the sound of someone packing a bag.

The only man she relied on and loved left the home, and she did not know if it was for a day or a lifetime.

Chapter 5

SYLVIE

France, 1996

Sylvie Tellier's early childhood revolved around her mother, Brigitte, whom she adored. Her father would often watch as they sat together for hours, tinkering in the kitchen or the garden and acting like they were the only two people in the world. When Monsieur Albert Tellier tried to get involved, too, he would get a hug now and then and not much more.

Sylvie devoured the typical flavours in the countryside: bulbous grapes and plums ripe for the taking all across the Dordogne, and kitchens smelt of the fresh local cheese bought by the kilo.

"You must learn English and French, Sylvie. It will help all your life, trust me."

Brigitte seemed to speak with a strange wisdom that made no sense to her daughter.

"Why would I, when I won't ever leave this country?"

She had no concept of a time when she might need to leave, so when her father announced that they were moving to Scotland, it felt like her world had imploded. At the age of sixteen, she was asked to pack up everything she owned and say goodbye to her friends and the only life she knew.

\#

Edinburgh, 1997

Less than three months later, the Tellier family arrived in Edinburgh. Sylvie watched all her belongings spill out of a lorry parked outside their new home.

She struggled to wrap her young tongue around some of the tricky Scottish consonant combinations.

"You must look for an opportunity, not for what is missing," said Brigitte.

Sylvie wasn't sure what that meant, but discovering that there was a fresh food market in Stockbridge cheered her up a little. The closest school was already full, so she was enrolled in the one next door — theirs was an area with a 'mixed demographic'. This was an English phrase she neither understood nor cared to anytime soon.

When the school bus came to pick her up, she would keep her head down and head for the nearest free seat. Staring out of the window and trying to navigate her new world, she noticed details. The faces at the bus stop. The loud, bright signs in shop windows. The girl who sat at the next bus stop was always in the same spot.

She just stayed there, fiddling with her hair. She was blonde, and so, so slim, and Sylvie felt frumpy in comparison; less feminine, somehow. The girl would board the bus and walk to the back, ignoring all the whistles and the catcalls the boys aimed at her. Her confidence intrigued Sylvie. It made her feel less afraid.

By day five, Sylvie had worked out that the girl's name was Ava, and that she was clever. In class, Sylvie watched as Ava answered questions with ease when others struggled. Even so, she still seemed disinterested in making friends.

At first, the painfully shy seventeen-year-old Sylvie just watched as Ava sat back quietly at her desk and completed the task in hand before putting down her pencil and folding her arms, bored, and waiting for the world to catch up.

Their sixth-form teacher wore a lot of cardigans and smelt of lavender soap, and Sylvie didn't like the way she looked at Ava.

What's she staring at? Does she think she's cheating?

Cardigan Lady seemed interested in punishing Ava's speed, though. She would try to dismiss it, like her intelligence and competence were irritating.

"Perhaps you could work through some past exam papers, Ava if you're finished? Or read a book?"

Sylvie watched as this mystical girl kicked back with a book she had pulled from her school bag. All around her, heads were being scratched and brains stretched.

Leaning forward as subtly as she could, Sylvie tried to glimpse at Ava's book. A slight sneer escaped her mouth, though, and alerted Ava of her presence.

"Eh. Can I help you?"

Sylvie shrunk back in horror, shamed at being caught. "Sorry. It's just—that's clever. I mean, your magazine..."

Lost for words, she pointed at the magazine perched inside the hardback that was resting in Ava's hands.

"Sorry, I mean—nice move!"

"Maybe not draw attention to it, then, yeah?"

"Sure, sorry, of course. I'm Sylvie, by the way."

By now, Ava was giving Sylvie her back, but she still managed to introduce herself. "I'm Ava. And I already knew your name."

"I used to read *Glamour* all the time in France."

It was a desperate and feeble attempt to impress the girl who seemed to have her life conquered.

"Good for you. It beats Shakespeare's comedies, that's for sure," she said. Ava was quick with words. "France, eh? Bet you're glad to have landed here instead, huh?"

Sylvie heard the sarcasm in Ava's voice and took it as an icebreaker.

"Do you know Michael's staring at you?"

Ava glanced toward the tallest boy in the class. Michael was two years older than the rest of them, and no one knew why he was there. He was both mysterious and handsome.

"Yes, he's a bit creepy."

"Do you think?"

Ava seemed bored already and kept flicking through the pages of her magazine.

"Do you want to have lunch together tomorrow?" *Oh God, that sounded so desperate.* "I mean, just grab a sandwich or something."

Sylvie couldn't help but pick up on Ava's cold   body language, as she refused to make eye contact when answering her questions.

"Um, okay, I suppose."

"Why d'you spend so much time on your own at lunchtime?"

The silence that followed shamed Sylvie a little. She heard Ava exhale deeply in what felt like a warning shot of overstepping the mark.

 "Sorry. That was rude."

"Dunno. I just — just like the peace, I 'spose. Most of these kids annoy me."

Intrigued, Sylvie pushed a bit more. "What? Really? Does that not get lonely?"

"Well, you're the same, Sylvie. What's your reason?"

She put a heavy emphasis on Sylvie's name, paired with an odd accent. It felt unpleasant.

"Well," she answered, "that's easy. It's because I'm, you know, the new girl. I'm from another country. People don't understand me and they think I can't understand them because I speak another language."

"We seem to have lost concentration here, class," Cardigan Lady said. It seemed like she lost her patience with the slow learners, and that her attention was on the back of the room now. "Could we have less talking and more doing, please?" After rolling her eyes, Ava went back to her magazine, leaving Sylvie to battle through her assignment alone. Still, Sylvie was buoyed by their connection.

The girls sat together at lunch the next day, and for the days that followed. While Ava didn't talk much, Sylvie was content to do the heavy lifting.

"What are you looking at? Can you not just eat your lunch, Sylvie from France?"

"Are you going to leavers' prom?"

"Um. I'm not sure, really."

They were sitting at the far end of a bench, keeping a safe distance from the boys.

"Why don't we get ready together beforehand? At my house?" Sylvie said, but Ava looked underwhelmed at the prospect. "Or, I could come to your house if you prefer?"

"Oh God, no. My parents are awful at the best of times. My mother would be unbearable before the prom."

"Okay. Come to mine, then. About six?"

In the short time she had known Ava, Sylvie hadn't once heard her talk fondly of her parents, but she was learning not to push for detail. She would just listen as Ava's story spilled out, waiting for each chapter to unfold.

"My dad is a control freak who thinks money can buy everything and my mum is a social climbing emotional vacuum."

Sylvie treasured every word and watched as this girl — the closest thing to a friend she had — walked home, a place of apparent misery. She could feel a sense of purpose growing within her. There was a loneliness in Ava that needed to be filled with something real. A relationship that mattered.

#

On the night of the prom, Ava arrived at Sylvie's house, late but unapologetic. Sylvie watched her coming through the front door from her vantage point at the top of the staircase.
"Ava! My dear. You look beautiful."
Sylvie felt a little embarrassed by her mother's welcome. Sometimes, it felt like she tried a little too hard to be the perfect host. She was relieved to see her retreat towards the kitchen and pull fresh food from her larder, mumbling in French as she worked.
"She's a bit starey sometimes, your mum — don't you think?"
By now, Sylvie was aware that Ava didn't tend to hold back her opinions. Ava was wearing a full-length scarlet gown, low cut with a sweetheart neckline; it was a figure-hugging dress, with a long slit on the left.
"Ah, *mon ami*! You look stunning! No wonder all the boys fancy you."
Ava didn't react, something that frustrated Sylvie and made her resent her friend's looks even more. She sensed tension, but couldn't understand it. Where was the prom night's excitement? The nervous giggles and pride in her undeniably stunning outfit?
"What's wrong, Ava?"

Ava simply made a show of being underwhelmed by the occasion and slumped down on Sylvie's bed.

"Nothing, I guess… but… let's just say, I think it's time to get this party started."

"I feel so frumpy compared to you. I knew I shouldn't have gone for the short dress; I don't have the legs for it. And I can't breathe with this waistband. What do you think?"

Ava opened her rucksack and pulled out a carrier bag. Sylvie could make out the contents at once and felt uncomfortable.

"Ava…"

"Chill out, Sylvie. You look great, and you'll feel better when you get some of this."

"Ava, I don't think we should."

"Oh, come on you. It's prom night."

"Yes, and my mum will —"

"Your mum's baking croissants or something. We'll be out the door before she has time to smell anything. Come on!"

Chapter 6

Edinburgh 1997

By the time they arrived at the prom, Ava was drunk, as she had worked her way through the hip flask hidden in her rucksack before leaving home. Sylvie, on the other hand, embraced her self-appointed role of protector. It gave her meaning, and it would distract her from not being invited to dance; it gave her a reason to go home early and for Ava to be grateful.

She'll thank me tomorrow. I know it.

And, as if taking on her own role, Ava looked determined to have the night she may regret.

"God, it's dull in here. Shall we shake up the dance floor, Sylvie?"

"What about something to eat instead?"

"Eating's cheating, didn't you know? I'm off to find the DJ."

"No, Ava, wait a second —   "

"Coming through, coming through, watch out losers!"

While she monitored her friend swaying towards the dancefloor, Sylvie noticed how Michael was loosening his collar and combing back his floppy fringe, as if he wanted to preen himself before approaching Ava. She saw Ava teasing him before moving along, and it pleased her on many levels, even if she didn't understand why.

Then Ava disappeared, lost in a sea of bodies and strobe lights, and just like that, Sylvie lost her purpose. It left her exposed, almost naked, and panicking. She started pacing around, past people who laughed, danced, flirted, and acted like young men and women of the world. Sylvie couldn't do any of that, though. Not when she felt unattractive and awkward.

The sight of Ava's scarlet dress cutting through a sea of dimly lit bodies pulled Sylvie out of her own darkness.

"Ava?"

Thank God.

Ava was near the door at the end of a corridor. Michael had found her again, it seemed, and they huddled together. She was still swaying, but Sylvie watched with resentment as Michael acted as a strong leaning post. They were talking in hushed tones, pointing towards the exit. They must have been planning something. Something risky. Whatever it was, it was bound to be a bad idea.

"Ava!"

Peering over her shoulder, Ava nodded in her direction, and that encouraged Sylvie to approach the pair.

"Ava? I was worried you—"

"Oh, look, it's your little French bodyguard."

"Shut up, Mike."

She could hear Ava swear under her breath. Her speech was slurred, and it made her sound like a stranger.

"What's up, Sylvie? Lost your girlfriend?"

Michael rubbed his hand on Sylvie's back before winking at her. The humiliation was intense, but she couldn't walk away.

"Ava? Can I borrow you just, just for a minute?"

"Go on, Ava, Mummy wants a word."

Michael's friends had joined in with supporting sniggers, making her feel smaller with every passing minute.

"Christ, Sylvie, what is it?" Ava asked.

Attempting to whisper to her friend, Sylvie did her best to cut through the drunken fog that was written all over her friend's face.

"What are you up to?"

Ava winked and held a finger to her lips, but gave her no other response.

"You're planning something. What is it? Where are you going with him?"

"Jeez, Sylvie. Can you just piss off and let me have some fun?"

Sickened to the core, Sylvie could just watch as the group headed for the cloakroom. She heard Ava's giggle fading in the distance when Michael pretended to trip her up by standing on her dress.

Then they were gone, until she caught sight of them again, tearing across the gardens.

Shit. What are you doing, Ava?

Sylvie knew that Ava was beautiful, and all the boys were attracted to her; she also knew that Ava was not interested in Michael, as he reminded her of her overbearing father. *He thinks he's the alpha male, just like Dad. But he won't win me over, that's for sure,* Ava loved to say before shunning him time and again.

Now Sylvie could only cringe at her attempts to protect Ava, watching as she leaned on Michael's shoulder. They were heading towards the riverbank.

Wetness seeped into her shoes when the heels sank into the lawn; still, she waited until her eyes adjusted to the dark. Sylvie feared this would not end well, but just watched as her friend carried on toward the sound of the water.

Other than Sylvie, the place was deserted. The riverbank was a spot the girls knew well, as they had spent hours there in the summer, leaping into the water to escape the heat of any rare Scottish sunshine. Michael had often loitered nearby, trying to muscle in on their time.

Every so often, a few droplets would hit Michael's face, lit up by the moonlight. He seemed full of longing, and she hated herself for admiring his profile, the way he held his head up high.

You're wasting your time, Michael. She's just drunk.

Edging closer to the waterfall, Sylvie kept her distance a little. She didn't want to be seen yet. Sylvie saw Ava's confidence, but also her vulnerability.

She watched as Ava dipped her toes toward the fast-flowing water below. Ava perched on their favourite spot — a patch of smooth rock overhanging the outer reaches of the waterfall. The girls had sat there together often, chatting about everything and anything they could think of. But not today. Reaching for Michael's arms to lean against, Ava seemed to block out the rest of the world. Sylvie was used to being in awe at the way her friend moved, but she sensed a lack of control in the moment, which unsettled her.

Ava stretched downwards, where a ridge jutted out of the water.

Careful, Ava, careful.

Too late. Sylvie could only watch as her friend slipped, unable to correct her fall as her foot snagged the hem of her dress. It billowed for a moment, its red fabric caught by a gust of wind, and then Ava was gone.

"Ava! No!"

Tearing her own shoes off, she scrambled towards the edge as fast as she could. Michael would get to Ava sooner, she knew it, but that didn't stop her from shouting.

"Michael, save her!"

The wind was howling, and she couldn't hear his answer. *Why is he still standing there?*

"Jump in, now!" she yelled again, but he was frozen to the spot.

Before Sylvie could think better of it, she reached the edge of the waterfall and lept in. The water felt like a million sharp blades were attacking her skin, but she pressed on. A streak of colour — red — floated towards a group of boulders ahead.

"Ava! Ava, I'm coming!"

The propulsion and energy Sylvie found within herself came from somewhere deep inside. She welcomed it and swam hard against the current with one end goal in sight.

It felt like forever before Ava's head broke the surface. Relief flooded Sylvie as she swam towards Ava, who was trying to stay afloat. A moment later, though, her head disappeared again.

Despite the current pushing Sylvie in a different direction, she forced herself to dive until she found a body — it was motionless and trapped near a partially submerged boulder. Ava's leg was tangled in something green, and her mouth was open in a silent scream.

Think, Sylvie. No, don't think. Just do something.

Seconds passed. Sylvie swam upwards to fill her lungs before going back underwater. It was hard to see something among the dense undergrowth, so she tugged and ripped at the seaweeds, ignoring her fading strength. She couldn't give up. At last, the soft but unmistakable touch of skin replaced the slimy sensation of the seaweed. Ava was free. Folding her arms under Ava's, she pulled until they both made it to the riverbank, then she must have fainted for a moment, because she came to at the sound of Michael's words.

"Shit. Shit. What do I do?"

Michael sounded odd, and there was a crippling pain in her abdomen. Opening her mouth to shout was overwhelming.

"Put her on her side!"

This was the easy bit, Sylvie thought as she staggered to where Michael stood. He was staring at Ava, transfixed like a marble statue.

"Jeez, what the hell?" he said when he looked up.

"Shut up, Michael, we're not losing her."

"No, you! Look—"

He was pointing to the pool of blood gathering below Sylvie. She assumed it was the reason for the pain in her middle, but there was no time to figure out what was wrong. Ava was lying lifeless in front of her.

Chapter 7

SYLVIE

Edinburgh 1997

Sylvie listened to Michael's desperate cries for help as she tried to keep her breathing under control. There was no one close enough to help them, though. It was why they loved the spot so much. Far enough from the school building to be hidden from view and sound.

Come on, Sylvie. You can't let her down now.

A memory of her own mum demonstrating first aid basics came to mind. It was always in her times of greatest need that Sylvie found herself drawn to her mother's teachings. Theirs was a bond that seemed to have no rough edges or imperfections. It was the truest source of comfort for mother and daughter.

"Do you know that kissing can keep someone alive?" she had told her then, injecting humour into most things as she often did. Sylvie had watched her mum in awe as she went through the life-saving motions with one of her dolls. Now it was no doll. It was something much more precious.

Two breaths, thirty pushes, two breaths and thirty pushes, what if I hurt her – two breaths – maybe it's twenty pushes? – two breaths, thirty – just keep going, Sylvie.

And then, a choking sound cut through the air.

Oh, thank God.

As she opened her eyes, Ava looked overwhelmed by the air and sunshine. The world seemed to be coming slowly back into focus as she turned her head in the direction of Sylvie's exhausted breaths.

Sylvie's whole body was aching now. Her clothes were bloody, but she wouldn't let go of Ava's hand as they lay on the water's edge. She had used all fear, anger, and determination to bring Ava back to safety. Watching her charge shift slightly next to her, Ava put a protective hand on her torso.

"Don't. Don't move too fast."

"Sylvie?" Her name sputtered out of Ava's lips. "Sylvie...?"

"It's okay, Ava. You're okay, now. Michael's gone to get help."

"What — did I?"

There was a sort of childlike relief written on Ava's face, something Sylvie had never seen before. They embraced until a coughing fit began again. Colour was returning to her cheeks, though, and she managed to sit upright.

"You saved my life," Ava said.

At that moment, Sylvie understood. This girl, body, and soul, felt like a part of her. She could not imagine a world where they were not there for each other. She wanted so desperately to tell her how much she cared about her. But it was obvious that Ava wanted to escape. To get out of there before they were caught.

"We have to get out of here."

"What?"

"Sylvie, we can't let anyone see us like this. My parents. They'll…" She coughed some more as water dribbled from her lips.

"Ava, calm down. You nearly —"

"Shit, someone's coming. Can you run?"

Sylvie sensed the panic in her friend's voice and gathered her strength. Two bright circles of light were moving towards them, accompanied by voices.

"We have to go now, please!"

They lent on each other to get up and stagger away. Putting one foot in front of the other, they blocked out what had just happened and went in search of a hiding place.

#

They made it back to Sylvie's house just before midnight, soaked and shivering. The bleeding around Sylvie's wound had stopped some time ago, but she knew that Ava needed to be seen by someone. Creeping upstairs, the two girls got into Sylvie's bedroom before shutting the door behind them. Sylvie desperately wanted to wake her mother up and seek comfort and reassurance that they would both be fine. Loyalty to Ava kept her quiet, though. While whispering in hushed tones, Sylvie began pulling out some warm clothes for them both to change into.

"Let's go to A & E, Ava. We have to get you checked."

"We can't. My Dad knows half the doctors there, and if he finds out what I was up to, he'll make me pay for it. I know it. He's desperate to show everyone that I can't cope on my own. Desperate to be right about me. That I'm a waster, a failure," Ava said, and Sylvie saw the fear and the pleading in her eyes.

"He's still your dad."

"Yes, and he thinks I can't do anything without him and his big, fat wallet."

"I don't get it."

"You wouldn't. Your family—your life is—" Ava pointed at Sylvie's middle. "Go to the hospital then. Get *that* checked over."

The gesture felt somehow demeaning. As if admitting her own pain would be akin to admitting weakness.

"I'm not going anywhere tonight. I need to look after you. Get changed now, before my parents wake up."

After throwing some clothes in Ava's direction, Sylvie went to check the bathroom cabinet. In there she found some painkillers and a bottle of *Savlon* she could use to treat her wound. It was throbbing and she could feel a strangely numb sensation from somewhere deep beneath her skin, but dismissed it and pulled the elasticized waist of her leggings gently up over the bruising.

Sylvie hated lying to her parents, but she knew it was either silence or full disclosure. There was no middle ground, but she couldn't bring herself to do that to Ava. It would be like a betrayal. Besides, she had been entrusted with a secret, and it made her feel powerful. Important.

She clung on to that feeling even after she went to bed. Listening to Ava shuffling in the sheets near her, she heard a tone in her friend's voice that was rare and precious.

"Sylvie? You still awake?"

"Uh-uh."

"Thank you."

Sylvie didn't reply, but she felt a warmth in her friend's words, something so rare and precious she had never heard before. Like she had ripped a mask of self-reliance off and showed her true self.   "I was a dickhead to you tonight, and then you saved my life. Why?"

She didn't have an explanation either. Why, indeed? So many answers, but the truest of them all was the one she was too ashamed to share.

Because I need you in my life, and I want you to understand that you need me, too.

"Did I?"

"You did, Sylvie. I owe you one. I really do."

Those words would never be forgotten.

Chapter 8

SYLVIE

Edinburgh, 1998

When Sylvie married Michael, it was — on a surface level, at least — the perfect solution. The match had everything. She was secretly thrilled when Michael gave up his pursuit of Ava and allowed herself to believe that they were a better match. Where Ava had sharp edges and unpredictability, Sylvie was happy to be more malleable. Ava lived in the shadow of her father and ran away from anyone who reminded her of him. "You're less trouble than your friend, Sylvie," he'd say, and she enjoyed it, dismissing Ava's early warnings as jealousy.

"Don't be flattered by him. He's too in love with himself to have time for anyone else. You know that, don't you?"

But time marched on, and with it, the girls' lives began to diverge. At first in small ways, but then the big stuff. Sylvie's loyalty to her friend never wavered. Secrets of the prom night were kept from Ava's parents and, against all odds, she got the grades to go to university in Glasgow. Sylvie was left alone without her friend and needed something.

Michael often happened upon Sylvie walking her dog while he was on his way to work. He was only in his mid-twenties, but he'd shot his way up the career ladder after securing an apprenticeship with one of Scotland's legal firms. Apparently, they attracted candidates straight from school when they showed a certain something, employed them in an administrative role, and supported them through their degree and apprenticeship.

"Uni life not for you, then?"

It struck Sylvie that his questions often felt more like statements.

"Guess not. Wanted to study business and open my restaurant, you know? Still might."

"Hm. It's some hard work running a restaurant - you know that, yes?"

He was right, of course, and it didn't take much to remind Sylvie of her comfort zone. Still living with her parents, her life felt slow, a world apart from how she imagined Ava's playing out. Ava was probably debating with her tutors and fellow undergraduates by day, and experimenting at night. With every term break, Sylvie dreaded how little she brought to their friendship: no stories; no tales of meaningless sex or smoking at parties. So, instead, she decided to devote her energy to the other thing she wanted — becoming a mother. Michael's confidence was irresistible to Sylvie, who felt her biological clock ticking in her ear. Less than eighteen months after their first date, Michael proposed during a holiday on the Isle of Arran, just off Scotland's west coast. They were watching puffins on the Isle of Arran, standing at the edge of a rocky beach, and Michael told her that he couldn't imagine spending his life with anyone else. At last, she had something exciting to tell Ava when she came home for Christmas.

"You, my precious Ava, you will be my bridesmaid, won't you?"

"Only if there is some handsome best man you can hook me up with!"

"No, seriously, I need you right there, by my side," she said. "Keep me from tripping all over myself with nerves. Will you?"

"Of course, dafty. Where else would I be?"

Sylvie was used to hearing Ava say that marriage was for people who had run out of their sense of adventure, for people who were needy. Why would you want to listen to someone else's opinion and pick up their dirty socks every day?

"You are so cynical, my friend. We should sort that out—or not. It means I'll never have to share you with another needy, sock-wearing man, then!"

Michael married her in front of a crowd; 150 people gathered at the Grand Hotel in Edinburgh, and it was, by all accounts, the perfect day. Except for one thing. Brigitte had died the year before, and Sylvie felt her absence all over again, like a raw wound that refused to heal.

At least she had Ava. She would always have Ava.

#

Sylvie had always wanted children. The need to be a mother crept up on her from as young an age as she could remember until one day it seemed to define her. Although she harboured dreams of owning her own restaurant, nothing felt more certain about her future than holding a baby in her arms. This showed in the way she behaved around children. Growing up in a home that was built around love and comfort caused her to long for a family of her own.

Her mother never spoke of the burden of parenting. Whether it was real or not, she managed to project the maternal role as a fundamentally rewarding one, immersed in joy.

The knowledge that Michael was excited about starting a family as well comforted her, even if she hadn't outright asked him about it. As it happened with a lot of other things, she just knew; he would often tease her, but she hoped they would agree on the important stuff— on how to raise their children, how to teach them right from wrong.

All her ducks were in a row to embark on the blissfully contented journey to parenthood that her own parents had enjoyed.

She secretly wished for the 'honeymoon baby' she read about in her romantic novels, but knew things didn't always happen right away and made light of it at first.

"Do you think we are doing it wrong?" she would joke after six months of trying.

"I think it's more likely to be something going on inside there."

They were soaking in the sun at Kelvingrove Park. It was a beautiful spring day, and Michael's words, as he pointed to Sylvie's abdomen, took her aback.

"What do you mean?"

"Well—you know, it's bound to be *female* problems, isn't it, my little French fancy?"

The way he laboured the word *female* felt insulting.

"Is it?" Sylvie shot back, not really thinking.   "Do you have no part to play in this process?"

"Well, yes, but it doesn't tend to be men that have the issues, does it?"

Sylvie looked at him and tried to ignore the knot that was rising up through her stomach at his words.

Michael had recently secured a job with one of the UK's top law firms, and he was on a steep trajectory toward his own world dominion. When it came to age-appropriate life goals, he had nothing to answer for.

"Maybe we should get, you know, checked?"

"Don't be ridiculous, Sylvie. You get *checked* if you want, but there's nothing wrong with me."

She just wanted to be reassured, but his words made her feel inadequate. Her husband was watching her as she picked a daffodil. They were already dying.

Don't spoil the moment, she thought. *Just let it go for now.*

"Heard it can take months after you come off the pill for your womb to settle into a new rhythm," she told him, the words tumbling out of her mouth by their own free will. "To be ready for — you know — action!"

She could handle fielding the odd question from her father and late mother's friends, and for a while, she didn't mind, happy to wait. Lately, though, the questions kept coming.

What colour of wool should they knit with? Hope you're enjoying your quality time as a couple – it won't last, you know?

Infertility is something that happens to other people, she believed on an unconscious level. As Michael said, her ovaries may not be doing their job as well as they hoped yet, but it would all be fine.

Just fine.

Hitting the one-year mark of trying to conceive — the official term now — felt different. She went through the ebb and flow of her moods as the months passed, the 'maybe this time,' followed by the gut-wrenching disappointment when the cramps came.

The rollercoaster of emotions was eroding their happiness, little by little.

"Michael, the doctor said we should take some tests."

"You really want to put yourself through all that poking and probing?"

"I just want to do what we need to, whatever the outcome."

"Christ's sake. Okay. I'll go for tests. Now, can we please talk about something else? I have a huge case to handle and, unlike you, I can't afford a life of leisure."

His words hit Sylvie like a sledgehammer. It had been his decision; he said he needed to know where she was, that she should look after the house since he earned enough for the both of them. Why was he resenting her now?

Maybe he was just stressed out. She would keep the peace, though, and everything would be better soon. That was her role, after all.

Still, she remembered his comments about women and conceiving. The belief that any man of any age would be able to father children angered her. The fact he had been smoking twenty cigarettes a day for years may not be helping matters either. Not that she would dare to share her thoughts on that. There were lines she could never cross.

Chapter 9

AVA

Glasgow Airport, 1999

The guard standing in front of the lounge had an air of patronising judgment that made Ava feel mischievous.
"May I see some ID, madam?"
"I'm meeting a friend inside."
"Lovely. If you give me your name and ID, I'll check if we have you on our list."
Dickhead.

"My name is Ava. My friend's name is Sylvie Tellier, and if you just give me a minute, I'm sure I can find my ID. My warrant card is in here somewhere."

Ava ferreted around her tote bag, hoping that her passport was among the lipsticks and chewing gums littering the bottom. Pretending to be a cop was a little game she liked to play on men with oversized egos, aided by her love of cop dramas; she loved the idea of being in control with only a badge and a pair of handcuffs.

The gamble with Dickhead paid off. Before she could find her passport, he shrank in himself.

"Apologies, madam. Please go right ahead."

"Ava! Here, sweetie, here!"

She spotted her friend at last, standing up from a large red leather chair and waving excitedly in her direction. It looked like she had been lost in the pages of some pretentious magazine that was thrown to one side.

"Christ, Sylvie, could you check your messages? Billy Big Balls wanted to send me packing to the departure lounge with the less entitled people."

"Oh, sorry, honey. I was just enjoying the courtesy bar. Got one for you too!" Sylvie said, raising a glass of bubbly. "Let's start like we mean it, yes?"

"You do know it's eleven in the morning, right?"

"Ah, that's midday in France, then. Perfectly acceptable."

Ava hesitated, but she felt increasingly tempted to go along rather than burst Sylvie's bubble. She lifted up the flute, which was filled with something pink and expensive-looking.

"Well, you know I wouldn't turn down a booze cruise, but I'm not sure I can afford it, Sylvie. Struggling to make rent as it is."

"It's on me, honey. And what on earth is a 'booze cruise'?'
"Oh God, you're so posh. A booze cruise is a trip with the sole purpose of consuming as much alcohol as possible."
"Hm, okay. Haven't you got a real job yet?"
Ava knew Sylvie had inherited a huge amount of money and that Michael was earning big, but she remained unimpressed. Her own father had cut off Ava's allowance after she failed her third-year exams. Having written off her academic potential in his mind, Ava lost faith in herself, and it showed in her results. But she was determined to succeed in life, with or without his help.
"That's really kind, but—"
"Please, Ava. I need this. I need you to myself for a few days, and I'm not too proud to pay for it."
"Ok, ok...you win. But if I end up not coming home again to face life's realities   , you can explain it to my landlord!"
Yes, Ava had other people's dissertations to write, deadlines, and overdue bills hanging in her wake, but something in Sylvie's voice rang alarm bells. She was fighting a private battle, a million miles removed from Ava's own troubles. There was no hiding from someone who has known you for more than a decade. And she didn't have the heart to turn her down. That's not the way their friendship worked. It had always been a symbiotic relationship. One calls, and the other answers. And this time it was Ava's turn to be there, where she was needed the most.

#

They stayed in a chateau owned by a family friend of Sylvie, and the rustic place, so small and intimate, felt perfect. They slept, wandered through the French countryside, had lunches and trips to the vineyards that dotted the region. Life was slow and hot. Hazy. Ava revelled in it, her bills a distant thought; and yet, something niggled at her. Memories of a drunken one-night stand kept surfacing.

Why? Why is it sticking to my mind?

She should be wondering whether the fitness instructor who made her laugh would call. She tried to remember the stories he told her about his *Bodypump* class, the light-hearted, fun stuff of a carefree life — she did, but —

A stomach-churning thought broke free.

Her period was late. Five days only, which meant nothing, obviously. Besides, they had been careful. She should forget about it. Get on with her holiday.

After taking a shower to rinse off the day's heat, Ava banished her worries and collected a bottle of white from the fridge before padding barefoot to the veranda. Sylvie was there, with her painted toes hanging from the hammock.

"There you are, *mon ami*. I do believe it's wine time!"

Ava was well aware that her poor attempts at French made Sylvie cringe every time, but there was no immediate reaction. A gentle afternoon breeze lowered the temperature and lifted the ends of her dress to her knees.

"Thank Christ it's cooled down a bit. You didn't warn me about it when you lured me here, did you?" she said.

Sylvie was staring into the distance as if lost in a trance. When no response came, Ava shook the hammock.

"Hello?"

"Oh, sorry, Ava. What were you saying?"

"Hot. This country is ridiculously hot."

"Ah, yes, I keep forgetting you lot can't take some heat. That's why your hair looks like that."

Ava turned sharply towards her friend, blowing the strands of hair out of her face and raising an eyebrow.

"Eh, remind me why we're friends again?"

Pausing between fake insults, they held up their glasses in a playful toast.

"So, tell me about married life."

"What, with the man that you rejected?"

"You know I wouldn't let just anyone have my sloppy seconds."

Sylvie sat upright in the hammock and the contents of her flute glass tipped slightly over the side.

"Why are you such an arse sometimes?"

"Oh, I'm only kidding," Ava said. "Maybe I'm a bit jealous, too—not of you having Michael, no, just of the whole *being settled with that special person* thing. Feel like I'll never get that, you know… what you have."

"What I have?"

A sobering look began to creep across Sylvie's face, which didn't go unnoticed by her friend.

"Ava, please, don't think it's all sunshine and roses."

Now that the bubbles were settling, Ava busied herself with refilling their glasses, intent on talking her way out of the niggling worry in her own head.

"You two seem so content to just have each other. You know…   I love that you're not rushing into starting a family, either. Probably wise to savour those first precious months."

The more Ava spoke, the more she realised that her words were not landing well. The look on Sylvie's face made her want to change the topic. She shouldn't have been making assumptions.

"Ava, that's not exactly what's going on here."

"Oh, shit, Sylvie, are you okay? Is everything all right with you and Michael?"

"Do I have to spell it out for you?"

Ava sensed a tone that was bordering on anger, briefly, before Sylvie regained composure and her expression softened as she lifted the glass to her lips.

"Don't ask me such questions when we're supposed to have fun!"

"Heck, what has that arrogant prick done this time?" Ava asked, going by her usual direct approach.

"That is my husband we are talking about!"

"I know. And you're my priority. Has he upset you?"

"We're fine! I guess things aren't always what they seem, sometimes."

"Sylvie. You know I struggle with philosophies when I'm three drinks in. Can you help me out here?" Ava said, and watched as Sylvie battled with herself and sensed her embarrassment.

"What sort of friend invites you on holiday just to launch into her own woes?"

"What do you mean? What woes?"

"Christ, Ava, it's not happening for me, is it? Pregnancy! Is it not obvious?"

Jolted back into her own fleeting thought of unwanted repercussions from a one-night stand, Ava wished for the ground to swallow her up. And then her own mind jumped to something that felt like selfish reassurance.

Of course you won't be pregnant after a one-night-stand. Here's evidence that couples are at it for ages before it eventually happens!
At least Sylvie was talking now, but still, she had work to make up for her tactlessness – fast.

"Sorry, I'm a big-mouthed arse."
Ava knew that it took a lot to offend Sylvie. They had known each other long enough for Sylvie to be very forgiving of Ava's lack of filter.

"I've told you that before," Sylvie said with a wry smile, before relenting.

"I guess life doesn't always go according to plan. We'd love a baby, but it's just not happening. I think there's something, you know, wrong with me."

"With you? For Christ's sake, Sylvie, you've been married less than two years. You just need to do it more."
While the words tumbled out of her mouth, the not unwelcome memory of her encounter with the Bodypump instructor hit Ava again.

Harmless fun, Ava, just be more careful next time, she told herself as the prosecco helped her to believe her own reassurance.
Next to her, Sylvie seemed to relax into a laugh. The relief brought by each other's company was palpable.

"Sylvie, you're my best friend and I'm here for you. You know that, right?"

"Of course, I do. The gloom can wait until we are back in Scotland, surrounded by clouds and grumpy people."

"Grumpy people? You French elevated grumpy to an art form."

Whether it was their mutual trust, the wine, or something else, Ava could not say. But she was aware that her tongue was becoming involuntarily loose.

"It's a minefield being single too, you know."

Sylvie looked a little confused by the comment.

"In what way? You and I are different, Ava. Always have been. Can't imagine you're in a hurry to settle down any time soon?"

Ava began to rock her hammock gently back and forward as she stared into the deepening red sunset.

"I had a one-night stand. And my period's late."

The smell of the countryside lingered as Ava avoided Sylvie's reaction and watched the sun disappear behind the horizon, leaving a trail of red and golden hues.

.

Chapter 10

SYLVIE

Edinburgh, 2000

Sylvie returned to a cold and dark Scotland and to a brown envelope, addressed to her but opened by her husband. He did that if he got to the mail first, and she accepted it. He was better at keeping their life and finances under control, so why would she complain? It meant she didn't have to worry about keeping on top of things that bored her, anyway.

This one mattered, though. The black NHS logo stood out, and it had to be the letter that explained it all. The reassurance she craved. Maybe they needed a few extra supplements or some medication to help move things along. Her road to happiness was on that small piece of paper.

"Don't I get a kiss after being abandoned for so long?"

Sylvie obliged and placed a hurried kiss on his cheek. "Is that from the hospital?" she asked then.

"Yep. Not worth wasting your time reading it, though."

"What do you mean?"

"I mean, it tells you nothing useful. Told you it was a waste of time going through all those tests. According to them, there's *nothing wrong with you.*"

He finger-quoted it as he spoke, and she cringed at his tone. It made her despise him.

"What about you?"

"What about me?"

"Your results. Have they arrived?"

"Yes, Sylvie. They have."

"And? Where's your letter?"

"What, *and*? There's nothing wrong with me either!"

His words were brutal. She wanted to see his letter. To see proof of what he was telling her.

"I don't understand. Let me see it," she said, stretching to grab the letter he'd propped against the fruit bowl. It was in full display as if he meant to torture her with it.

"Michael, don't be like this. I just want answers. Don't you?"

"Sylvie, these doctors — you hold them on such a high pedestal, but they don't always know everything."

"What do you mean?"

"Well, it's obvious. You're just not the childbearing type, it seems. They can't write that in a letter now, can they? Mother is a bit, well, defective!"

He chuckled a little, satisfied by his own humour while Sylvie's heart sank through the floor. Grabbing the letter to see the truth for herself, she started skimming it.

— the results have delivered no definite cause for further investigation. At this stage, we can offer no obvious reason for your failure to conceive and determine a diagnosis of unexplained infertility. Please be aware, there are still many options open to you at this stage. If you would like to make an appointment at our Infertility Clinic, our team would be delighted to discuss them with you —

Sylvie crumpled into a large leather armchair, defeated and lost.

"Perhaps we're just not biologically compatible, or something?" Sylvie told her husband as she drowned her sorrows inside a bottle of Merlot, searching for an explanation that would settle her mind.

"Don't be ridiculous. I don't want to talk about this anymore tonight. Some of us have work to do. Living in a flat like this doesn't happen by accident."

Sylvie knew there was going to be less and less room in her world for anything other than *this*; the all-consuming, relentless fertility battle. It was already sapping at her energy, her time, and in the end, it would rip out her heart. Still, she kept hoping, even if her dream of a home bursting with chaos and noise and smelling of fresh baked bread faded around the edges.

She waited until Michael had slept his mood off before approaching him again. It had been bad timing on her part. She had only just got back, and the house needed to be tidied up the way he liked. Things had got messy in her absence, and she knew it troubled him. She observed him as he sat on his favoured side of the sofa, legs outstretched and a glass of single malt whisky in hand; then she padded closer, clutching at the IVF brochure.

"Michael, I have an idea. I want you to just consider this." He looked up, and she knew he was warning her to think carefully before she spoke. After handing over the brochure, Sylvie took a deep breath.

"What's this?"

"It's just a brochure — about our options."

"What?"

"Our options. You know, assisted conception. It's called IVF, and I think we should consider it."

Michael didn't even look at the front picture; he didn't see the perfect-looking couple smiling at their infant. He just put it on the sofa beside him, as if she'd handed him some junk mail, and then he closed his eyes.

Should she just stand there, watch him in silence? Should she say something? No, that wasn't wise. She could see that his anger had returned; there was a darkness within him that scared her.

"Michael?"

"No."

"What do you mean? When did you lose the will to fight and make our family complete?" she asked, but she regretted her bravery right away.

"Lose? Are you suggesting I'm the kind of man who gives up? Some sort of failure now?"

"No, of course not. That's not what I meant. I just can't bear to—"

"Do you think you could find a better option out there, Sylvie? A more appropriate sire for your offspring? Someone who can provide this lifestyle and make you happy?"

"Stop it, Michael, please."

The sickness Sylvie felt in the pit of her stomach was getting replaced by a dizzying sensation. What was this, some sort of panic attack? She felt unsure about her next breath, about the words that would come out of her mouth.

"Let it go, now," Michael told her.

"I don't know how to. I just found out that Ava—she's pregnant. After some trashy one-night stand. Just like that. She gets *my* dream."

She could see how much her desperation disgusted him. He'd often told her there was nothing worse than being a victim, after all.

Something had broken through his disinterest, though. Sylvie watched as he got to his feet and went to stare out of the window. Then he picked up his coat and left, leaving her alone with a few words as an explanation. A long walk, he had said. To clear his head.

Fine.

Fighting the thought, *why me?* that kept coming back was a little easier with the help of another glass of Merlot. It helped her drift into a world where the edges were less sharp and her pain dulled.

Why?

She had almost reached a place of comfort when a sound tore at her ears with a gnawing familiarity.

"Wake up, Sylvie. Pull yourself together."

She hadn't heard Michael coming back home, but the harshness of his voice tore her from her dozing. She did not know what time it was or when Michael returned home, but even through the haze, she detected something different about him. A renewed energy.

"Where did you go?"

"For a walk, just like I told you."

"I need to go to bed, Michael."

"Yes, you do. And you need to stop drinking so much."

Shame filled her, but it was what she deserved. "I'm sorry," she said. "I'm just—I'm just sad and angry."

"And what good will that do to you? To us?"

Keeping her head bowed, she managed a slight shrug. "Just let me rest, please. I'll feel better tomorrow."

"I take it as you don't want to hear my plan, then."

"Your what?"

"My plan, Sylvie. I have a plan for me and you to become parents, and you're going to love it."

Chapter 11

AVA

Edinburgh, 2000

Ava spotted the worrying signs right away. She knew Michael was an arrogant prick, and she also caught some tell-tale behaviours — the awkward silences between him and Sylvie in public, the constant jibes. She'd tried to hint at it at first, dropping comments about them forgetting to have fun, but it had fallen on deaf ears.

"Why don't we go to the cinema and see that new Tom Cruise film? He's still got it, don't you think?"

"I can't. I'm on day ten."

"Day ten of what?"

"My cycle. I could be ovulating soon. I can't risk, you know, missing the moment."

"Christ, girlfriend. You're telling me your egg hasn't even popped out yet and you can't even risk a trip to the cinema? Right, I'm coming to you tonight then. And I'm bringing chocolate."

Ava knew what an obsession looked like. There was always something to avoid or something that was required, like a given amount of sleep. Apparently, *living* was too risky for your potential child-rearing sanctuary. Despite her non-existent medical knowledge, Ava believed that such relentless pressure was unlikely to help.

And yet, Ava had her own mess to deal with, and the cruel irony and the subsequent chasm it created between them was not lost on her.

She was around eight weeks pregnant now, struggling to make ends meet, but hell would freeze over before she asked her dad for help. No, there was only one person she trusted, one who wouldn't judge her no matter what.

#

When Ava arrived at Sylvie's door that night, she knocked so hard that the neighbour's dog started barking. No sign of Sylvie, though, and her heart beat faster in her chest.

"Sylvie, I'm here. Are you decent?"

After letting herself in, she heard a cork popping and took a long, relieved sigh. *Thank God,* she exhaled as she stepped into the kitchen. Her friend was there, at least. That was enough reassurance. But the scene that greeted her was at once sad and lonely. Sylvie looked lost in whatever world the wine had taken her and didn't notice Ava arrival   .

"Oh, girl. What's going on here?"

Sylvie turned around a little too fast and lost her balance. To keep herself upright, she had to grab onto one of the bar stools.

"He — he dumped me, that's what!"

"He did what?"

"Yup, you heard me. Michael. He left me. Well, that's not strictly true, but not so far off, either," she said, her hand opening and closing as if to mimic her words. "Dumped, dumped, *dumped —*"

"Shit. Steady on, let me make you a coffee, and then you can tell me what the dickhead has done this time."

"Anyway." Sylvie looked her up and down. Somehow, it made her feel ugly. "How are you? Are you puking already? Worked out who the dad is?"

Ava raised her eyebrows. "Really? Sylvie, how much did you have to drink?"

"Shit, sorry, Ava, sorry. That was cruel. Maybe you fancy a dance?"

Ava watched as Sylvie started dancing by herself. It reminded her of drunk people at the end of a wedding when the party's over and no one wants to tell them.

"Not tonight. I just wanted to talk to you. You're so good at making me feel —"

"A little less shit about yourself."

"Okay, I think I should go. I'll come back tomorrow."

"No… sorry, Ava. Sorry. I've just had some bad news."

"Michael will come back, trust me. That man would be useless on his own; even though he's an arrogant dick, I'm pretty sure he needs you more than you need him," she said. "What happened anyway?"

Sylvie giggled. "You know, I'm not even sad about him leaving, or threatening to, or whatever. It's not even that."

"What then? What is it?"

"Turns out he was right."

"How so?"

"I'm defective."

Rage was building inside Ava's, but she clenched her fists and held it back. "Well, that's a word I've not heard in a few decades. You're what?"

"My womb. Well, actually, not my womb. My tubes. They're all bust up, it seems. Here's a tale for you, Ava. Are you ready?"

Ava caught sight of the fertility papers strewn across the table. Wine stains covered them. "Talk to me, Sylvie. Tell me what you mean by that."

"It's simple, really. Remember that day? At the waterfall?" Uneasiness crept up on Ava, and she nodded. "What, prom night? You know I'd never forget it."

"I hurt myself too. I bled a lot, if you can recall it." Sylvie's eyes were red. It was hard to tell if it was because of tears or too much alcohol. "Well, turns out the little tumble I took after rescuing you left me with lesions on my tubes. And the actual killer? It's game over for making babies. As in, not now, not ever."

Sylvie drew her hand across her own throat before pointing downwards.

"Bit crap, isn't it?"

No. This can't be happening.

Ava opened and closed her mouth several times, but no answer came. Nothing she could bear to say out loud. She sat down instead and counted up to ten, and waited for the racing in her heart to settle before she spoke again.

"Oh God, Sylvie. And Michael heard this and abandoned you?"

"Haha! Not so quick, my little detective. Oh no, Michael — Michael has a *plan*!"

"A what?"

"Michael, the man of the world that he is, came up with an excellent plan. Do you want to hear it?"

Ava didn't, but it felt like the only thing she could do. So, she nodded, and let Sylvie continue.

"I told him about your predicament, you see. I was a bitter cow when I heard that. Did you notice, by the way? Probably not. I hid it quite well. But Michael… well, Michael *thought* we should persuade you to be our surrogate parent. You know, for that child you are carrying, the one you neither planned nor wanted. There, you see. How do you like the sound of that?"

The smell of alcohol was making Ava nauseous, and she fought off an overwhelming desire to run outside and throw up. Anything to escape the moment she found herself in.

"Sylvie, I don't know what —"

" — The problem with men like my husband, as you probably know already, is that they can never understand why their perfect plans don't sound so perfect to other people."

"What did you tell him?"

Pausing only to refill her glass — she poured until not a single drop of Merlot remained in the bottle — Sylvie took a deep breath before speaking again. Her voice was full of determination. "I told him to piss off, of course. What else could I say?"

Who was this woman? Ava wondered. Where had she found the confidence to stand up to someone like Michael, who had squirmed his way into her life all those years ago? The man who had chipped away at her confidence, piece by piece — and yet. Somehow, faced with such a hideous solution, she had found the strength to say no.

Maybe it had been because of everything they went through together. For the fears and the secrets they shared. In that moment, Ava realised she had a deep respect for this fragile woman; she and Sylvie were so similar in so many ways, but also very different.

Her next words surprised them both.

"You should have said yes."

Sylvie looked up at her friend, through her own long, brown, silk eyelashes. Desperate for respite from the magnitude of what was passing between them, Ava remembered how she had always been jealous of those. She knew there would never be a mascara good enough to replicate them. Cosmetic beauty couldn't distract her for long, though. Sylvie's words forced her back into the moment.

"What did you say?"

"I said you should have agreed with him."

Ava watched as Sylvie slammed a glass down onto the kitchen worktop, unable to read her expression completely. Was it anger?

"Are you fucking mad? This is your child, Ava."

"I know that. But you saved my life, and it ruined yours."

"You're so dramatic sometimes."

"No, there's nothing dramatic about it. It's just a fact, just like the fact that Michael will never put himself through IVF. Far too much of a stigma for him, I bet."

Ava understood her friend's husband more than she wanted to. It often made her boil with anger that Sylvie was so blinded and flattered by the attentions of that man.

"He, he said, *'There's nothing wrong with my swimmers, so why the hell should I put myself through that?'*"

"Do you want to be with him for the rest of your life?"

"It's not that simple."

"Why not?"

"Because we weren't all born beautiful and confident like you. Michael may be far from perfect, true, but he found something in me, and it made him want to protect me. To look after me and be my husband. I don't believe I'd find that again, and I'm not built to be alone."

"You don't know that. Why do you always sell yourself short? Why the hell didn't you just look after yourself that day and forget about me? Then, then you wouldn't be in such deep shit now, and I wouldn't feel like I feel."

"Ah, but then I wouldn't have you in my life anymore; and that, my darling, is something I couldn't bear."

"You were fearless, Sylvie. You are a fighter — I'm going to make you see that."

"Yes, but you can't fix this. It's over and I need to face it."

Ava heard the sadness in Sylvie's voice and felt her pain as if it were her own.

"You should have agreed with him, and you still must. Because there is something I haven't told you yet."

Chapter 12

SYLVIE

Edinburgh, 2000

"I'm having twins."

The words fell from Ava's lips like they were nothing, but Sylvie felt how her body shook upon hearing them.

"What did you say?"

"You heard me. Twins," Ava repeated. The words felt so cold. So matter of fact, and left Sylvie winded, unable to form a proper sentence.

Say something. Anything. Congratulate her -that's normal in this situation.

"Wow. Ava, Ava, that's—are you okay?"

Ava fell silent, leaving it to Sylvie to fill the silence.

"Thought you were putting the kettle on? I'm still waiting, you know."

"What?"

"Tea? Do you want a cup?"

"Sylvie, please, sit down and look at me. Look me in the eye."

She did, she forced herself to, and what she saw in Ava's scared her. Ava had the look of someone who had stumbled upon an unknown part of themselves.

"I get it. Two babies. It's a shock, but you'll be fine."

"Stop talking, for Christ's sake. Stop and listen to me. I need to say something, so just be quiet."

By now, Sylvie was watching her closely, trying to read what would come next. She had a fair idea already, but, regardless; she needed to pretend otherwise.

"You're going to think I've lost it, or that I'm desperate and not thinking straight. But, you see—everything could—listen to me, please."

"What? What is it? You're scaring me."

"Just hear me out. I told you I have two babies on the way, and the thought of having one is overwhelming enough. Don't get me wrong. I know how lucky I am—I do."

"Listen," Sylvie began.   She needed to let her talk and play the part of the blindsided friend. "Listen, I get it. I don't resent you Ava, really, I don't. You know me better than that."

"Stop and listen to me."

A strange surge of terror and excitement rose inside her. Ava kept talking.

"We both know you were born to be a mother, Sylvie. Probably more than me, and definitely more than I was born to be a mother of twins."

"Ava? What are you saying?"

"I'm saying there's a way to live the life we both want and need."

"Don't be ridiculous."

Sylvie knew that twins were not in Michael's plan. She felt lost without his lead. But still heard the darkness of his words in her ears, even when he wasn't there.

"Sylvie, it's not ridiculous, it's perfect. I can carry them both, but we raise one each as our very own."

The women looked at each other as Sylvie let a million thoughts and hopes flood in.

"Have you thought this through?"

"Thought what, Sylvie? It can be as simple or as complicated as we want it to be. Think of it as a life for a life, if you like."

"I have never asked you to repay me for anything."

Make her believe it is her idea, remember that Sylvie. Let her do the pushing, and you just relent.

Sylvie was carrying out Michael's orders, even in the face of a curveball they hadn't predicted. This will please him, surely.

"Just tell me you're considering it."

Ava's words were almost pleading in tone. Almost as Michael had predicted.

"Considering it? I can't even process what it means. It's too huge."

"It makes sense, instead. You see that, don't you? Consider it a surrogacy arrangement. It happens all the time. This one is just a bit different. We will raise them in different homes, but close enough they'll be together from the start."

Don't mess this up. Make this work. You deserve it. We deserve it.

"This is the life of twins we're talking about. Your twins. You don't share them like sweets, no matter how desperate I am."

"I know. But it just—it just feels right. This happened for a reason. I mean, we have always looked after each other, you know, saved each other—literally, in your case. Please, let me do this for you."   Ava was begging now.   "We have to look after each other, remember?"

"I remember. I just never imagined it would be like this."

In the exchange of those precious and desperate words between Ava to Sylvie, their need for each other became written in stone.

Chapter 13

AVA

Edinburgh 2006

Sean agreed to meet Ava in the park. He was staying with his
mum outside Edinburgh, as he needed space and time to
think. They told Catherine that Daddy was going to look after
Granny for a while and she didn't question it. Explanations
can be simple when you're six.

"She misses you, Sean."

It was a fresh March day, and crocuses had erupted across the
grass. It would have looked magical on any other day, but
neither of them felt like enjoying the scenery.

"Catherine needs her dad. Please, come home."

He pulled his collar up and rubbed some dampness from his nose. Surely those weren't tears. She couldn't bear to think of Sean that upset.

"I miss her too," he said. "But you don't just reveal something like this and expect life to go on as usual."

"Sean, you have to understand. I was on my own. Debts up to my eyeballs. It was a one-night stand, and I had no one, nothing except Sylvie. She was my world."

"Okay, and I get that. Still, there's quite a jump between being there for a friend and, and giving her your child!"

"She was having problems conceiving. Her and her husband. This man, Michael. I've known him almost all my life. He's— anyway, never mind. They'd been trying for years to have a baby, but it just, just didn't happen."

Sean was staring across the horizon. He looked lost in his thoughts and Ava wasn't even sure if he was still listening or not. She had to plow on, though, and make him understand.

"I've heard about people struggling to have babies before. But it's different when you see it in the eyes of your best friend. It takes on a reality that you can actually feel yourself. Does that make sense?"

"Lots of people have problems like that, Ava. It's not your responsibility to make it right. It wasn't your fault."

"Well, that's just the thing."

"Oh, what now? What more are you hiding?" Sean's tone was desperate. He looked haunted and Ava couldn't make eye contact anymore. They were approaching a park bench and Ava saw her chance to make him really listen.

"It was my fault, you see. Sean, please, stop walking and sit down."

"No. It's too cold. I need to keep moving," he said. "Go on."

"When we were kids… well, young adults, I guess, there was an accident. It was school prom, and I was drunk. Really drunk, and really stupid."

"Ava, where is this going?"

"I had a horrendous accident. Nearly drowned, because I was drunk and showing off. And Sylvie, she jumped into the river. It was reckless. Reckless and stupid, and so, so brave, Sean." She paused and looked at him. "I was unconscious, and she brought me to safety, but she hurt herself in the process. And the wound — it caused problems, you know, female problems."

"No, Ava, I'm a man. What do you mean, *problems*?"

"She didn't know back then because she didn't get herself checked out. That was my fault too. I was trying to cover it all up, you know. But she found out that the trauma had lesioned her fallopian tubes, which meant —"

" — That she couldn't get pregnant. I get it now. I understand."

"She saved my life, and I ruined hers, Sean. It's all my fault."

"Christ. So, this was your idea? The baby? I thought you said it was because you were broke?"

"I was. And I was a stubborn idiot who refused to run back to Daddy."

"And what, she made you an offer you couldn't refuse?"

"No, Sean. No. It wasn't like that. It started out as a drunken conversation, then it grew as the months passed. It was my suggestion, though. There's no getting away from that."

"People commit to running marathons when they're drunk, or they get a tattoo, or text an old boyfriend to tell them they're a knob, but not this! They don't give up a child." His anger seemed to grow. "How is that even legal? To split up twins at birth. Surely there are laws to prevent it?"

"I researched it all, and I found out it could begin as a private foster agreement, then move to formal adoption. Michael is a lawyer. He kept track of everything."

"Sounds like this Michael took quite the leading role."

Ava paused and let his words sink in. She had never trusted Michael, not really, but he had been there; right place, right time. Neither of them had the strength to question his guidance back then. They seized his strong and directing hand willingly.

Ava noticed the hard veneer of anger on Sean's face gave way to something softer, something that was beginning to resemble sympathy. She felt at ease for the first time in years. She knew that she had unleashed some almighty turbulence in both their lives and Sean had the right to react in any way he chose. Still , for Ava, there was a strange sense of release that came with the moment. Things were about to get complicated, and it made her feel more alive than ever.

"Sean, please, talk to me. I need to know how you feel."

"...How I feel?"

Her heart sank. "I haven't told you about it, and it's unforgivable, I know. I just... I guess, I just thought it would be easier if you didn't know until you absolutely had to."

"And now — why now, Ava? Why is it time for me to know?"

Answering that would feel like being shot twice. She kept going. "We were supposed to keep the girls close, so they could know each other as they grew up. Just as friends. I found out they wouldn't be identical, and I hoped they wouldn't attract attention until they were old enough to know the truth. To understand their true connection."

"So, let me get this right. You and Catherine have been meeting up with her twin behind my back? For years?"

"No, no. That's not what I'm trying to say. Things didn't go as planned."

"No shit. What were the chances, Ava?"

Sean's voice was loud enough to attract attention. Ava winced as she sensed the stares people were casting their way; they were probably thinking it was yet another run-of-the-mill domestic argument.

"Michael… it was his idea, apparently. He thought it would be better if they left Scotland after the adoption. He, he forced them to move to France, he must have convinced Sylvie somehow. A magical return to her home country or something, I think. He's always had a stranglehold on her," she said. As she talked, Sean dropped down on a bench and pressed his hands against his forehead, as if trying to protect himself from her tale. He wasn't fond of dramatic gestures, and Ava knew his pain was genuine.

"I heard no more from her after that. No photos, no cards, nothing, just like they fell off the face of the earth. It was awful, Sean, but I managed to bury it — bury my memories and thoughts of them and their life, so that I could get on with my own."

"And I'm asking again, Ava. What's different now? What changed?"

While his face was still made of hard, sharp edges, he was hanging on every word. She had to give him as much as she could now.

"They've returned. I heard his name on the radio, he's some fancy lawyer, and he's working on a case that hit the news. Some overpaid footballer caught with his pants around his ankles."

"Well, he sounds like he could use some work on his moral compass, anyway."

"Yes, but I want to find them. I want Catherine to meet her twin. She needs it."

"Jeez, Ava, can you give me half a minute to process all this before ploughing ahead? We are a family, you know."

"Are we? Still? I thought after you left... I didn't know when you would..."

"I just needed space to think. I love you both more than anything in the world, but this is hard. You've had six years. I've had six days."

"Yes, yes. Of course, I'm so sorry. It's—I guess I don't think it's going to go away this time."

"This time? What's not going to go away? The part where you introduce our daughter to the twin she didn't know existed or the part where you come to terms with seeing your own child again for the first time in six years?"

"I know. All of it. I've thought about this moment so much, I've had all these dreams about seeing them again. My mind just won't let it rest."

"How can this have been going on in your head, yet you've never told me? I thought we were a team. How can you have kept this from me?" he said.   "Catherine is only six years old, Ava. And you really think we should land this on her now? Her emotions are all over the place. This could be too much you see that."

By now, they were sitting face to face on the cold metal bench. Their hands were linked together, and they united once again.

"I know, but after I had that near miss. You know, in the car and then finding the drawings, well. It really made me think. Everything came flooding back.   What if I were not there?   You wouldn't have even known any of this. And, if you found out from Sylvie, you would have to make these decisions without me. I would have no part in how this played out, and the mere idea breaks my heart."

"It's a gut feeling, Catherine needs this. And I miss my friend. I really do."

"Maybe we should give it some more time? Just to be sure, we're not jumping into something like this. Why are you so convinced Sylvie would want to hear from you, anyway?"

"I don't. In fact,   it's more likely that she won't. But, I knew this day would come and I have to face it."

Ava saw the look on her husband's face and felt the enormous gulf that had opened up between them. A gulf filled with lost trust and disbelief. She felt an overwhelming need to explain and defend herself to the man whose opinion she cared about.

"I'm certainly not the same person I was seven years ago. Do you even remember what it feels like to make decisions that are instinctive?"

"Impulsive, you mean."

(Ava wondered if his resistance was just a test. He so often played the role of devil's advocate in the face of Ava's impetuosity.)

"I think Catherine's old enough for this,   but I want us to go down this road together, as a family, rather than wait until she finds things out by accident. I think we… I think I owe her that."

She could see the look on her husband's face that screamed, *this scares the hell out of me, but you've made your mind up and there is nothing I can do to stop you.*

"Don't you worry that Catherine seems quite lonely at school?" she added.

"She's just finding her feet, Ava. They all change friends every week at that age, don't they?"

"It's easier for boys. They can just kick a football about in the playground and not really have to worry about   best friends and all that girly baggage."

"I love you and I'll support you if this is what you want to do, Ava, but be prepared. It may not work out the way you intended."

Ava's heart hurt with love and guilt. Her husband was wrestling with his instinct to stand by her side, and all she felt was empowerment.

#

By the time they got back home, Catherine was poking around in the kitchen cupboards, leaving a trail of cereal, jam, and milk behind her. Their seventeen-year-old neighbour who had been watching her was only interested in the promised twenty pounds, it seemed.

"Mum! You're early! I wanted to make you a special lunch!"

"Oh, I am sorry, my love. Look who I brought with me!"

The mere sight of Sean was enough to send Catherine into a tailspin of excitement.

"Daddy! Is Granny well again?"

Ava's heart ached a bit as she faced the familiar parental torture of seeing their child grow too fast.

There was something about Catherine's self-sufficiency that felt to Ava as if she had let her down.

The ghost of her own mother haunted her still and she would not fail in her role as ultimate provider and healer, of all things. Taking on extra client work was helping to boost their household income when Sean's work had slowed down, but it left so little time for those trips to the zoo, park, or many other of those special moments. The stuff that 'Facebook Memories' are made of. Ava tortured herself with visions of how her friends' parents filled their time together with a multitude of rich experiences that Catherine did not get.

"She is loved, provided for, kept safe, and well fed. The rest is just padding," Sean would say, trying to reassure her.

Ava remembered her own childhood meals. She would get up early enough each morning to hunt in cupboards for a piece of bread to toast or a packet of biscuits to fill her tummy while her mother slept upstairs. A deeply bitter woman, Ava's mother had the inability to show her love in any practical or emotional sense. It made her constantly on the lookout for signs that her own daughter was keeping something inside.

"Catherine. Are you happy at school?"

"What do you mean, Mummy?"

"Do you have, you know, good friends and all that? People to have fun and play with?"

Catherine took a seat at the kitchen table and eventually began messing around with the food around on her plate. "Most of the time," she said. "Sometimes they aren't kind, but I just walk away, as you told me to, Mum."

"Not kind?" Ava's hackles rose. "What do you mean by *not kind*?"

"Well, there's one girl—Sammy—she's in Primary Four and keeps picking on some of the Primary Three at break time. Last week it was Rebecca, but Rebecca has a sister in Primary Six who saw it and said some scary stuff to Sammy. So, she left Rebecca alone after that." "Catherine, does anyone ever stick up for you?"

"Not really, but I try to, Mum. Like you've told me, good friends think of others first. Once Rebecca lost her packed lunch, and I shared mine with her—even my chocolate biscuit—and it made her happy again."

"I bet it did, sweetheart. I bet it did."

Guilt ate at Ava. Catherine was not a great sharer, and this was the first time she'd heard something like that. *How could I not know this?* she thought. *How long has it been going on for? What has been happening in my daughter's life that I have missed?*

"Catherine, please, promise me you will always tell me if you're lonely or unhappy at school. It's okay to feel that way and I want to help you feel better. I know Mummy is often busy, but I would always make time for you. You know that, yes?"

Catherine looked at her mother with a mixture of concern and gratitude, then reached out for a hug.

As they were tidying up together, Sean reappeared in the kitchen and lifted Catherine up for a cuddle, making her squeal in delight.

"It looks like a splendid afternoon for a trip to the park. Do you fancy hanging out with me while Mummy rests, my little wee one? "

"Yes, Daddy, *yes!*"

Within minutes they were at the front door, throwing on coats and scarves before heading out into the world.

As they left, failing to close the door behind them, Ava could still hear them talking.

"Is Mummy okay?"

"Of course, she is, honey. She just needs a bit of sleep and she'll be grand. Now, where are we going? Your choice! I've heard there are some hungry ducks on the hunt for the finest Peterson family stale bread."

Ava knew she should go straight to bed while she had the rare opportunity to get some sleep, but she also knew there was too much swirling in her own head. She had to write the letter that she'd revised in her own head so many times before. If Michael was back in Scotland, there was a chance that they were with him.   Where, though? She had to find some answers.   Catherine deserved to know she was far from alone in the world.

Her home office was a chaotic mess of screens, papers, pens, a digital radio, several empty glasses, and mugs. She sat down, pulled on the threadbare slippers that she always left under her desk, and began writing. The old-fashioned way. Pen to paper with no opportunity for deleting or re-writes. It was a letter that she knew was half therapy, half genuine correspondence. For now, it didn't matter that she didn't know where to send it. All that mattered was getting the words down.

Dear Sylvie,

I don't know whether this letter will reach you at a good time, but I wanted to start by saying how much I miss you and that I think about you and Josie almost every day. I' m aware   Michael is back in Scotland, which means   you are too, I hope. But, I need you to know —

We are ready, and I hope with all my heart that you are, too.

Chapter 14

SYLVIE

Glasgow, 2007

It was a beautiful spring day, and the Miller household seemed full of contentment, privilege, and innocence. Sylvie's child revelled in the simple joys of playing with her dolls, clasping them in her soft, delicate hands, and bringing them to life under her mother's gaze.

"They're sisters, Mummy. They are going to live together forever, and ride ponies all day."

"That's sweet, darling," Sylvie said, ignoring the sting of those words.

"You help me give them names, Mummy! Mummy — Mum!
I'm talking to you!"

"Sorry, Josie, I was miles away."

It wasn't the first time that Sylvie got lost in her own head.
Sometimes her daughter's happiness became overshadowed
by a darkness she could not escape, and her mind drifted.

"Why won't you play with me properly? Are you sad?"

"No, my angel, I'm never sad when I'm with you. I was just
wondering when Daddy might be home. Would you like to
help me make dinner? I'd love that."

"Okay, let's make happy food. Like you do for me when I get
lonely."

Sylvie knew that the veil of bliss she pulled over her life to
benefit Josie would crack soon — perhaps too soon. For now, at
least, they remained the centre of each other's lives as they
prepared home-grown vegetables in their elegant kitchen.
Today, Josie was shelling peas.

"Mummy?"

"Yes, darling?"

"Were you ever sad that you didn't have a brother or sister to
play with?"

"Maybe I was, Josie. But when you never have something, you
don't really miss it, do you? Why are you asking me this? Are
you sad?"

"Not really. I have friends at school to play with. Did you
have friends,   Mummy?"

Sylvie laughed at the directness of the question. Even at the
tender age of seven, her daughter had developed an ability to
get straight to the point.

"Yes, I   did, angel. I had one very special friend."

"What did she look like?"

"Well, she was very pretty. She had long, blond, curly hair and a few freckles on her nose."

"She sounds like a princess! I've got blond curly hair too. Maybe I'll be a princess one day?"

"You're already our princess, remember? Like Daddy tells you."

"Is she not still your best friend?"

How does she do this to me? Sylvie thought. "Well, unfortunately, I don't see her anymore, darling."

"Did you have a fallout?"

"No, Josie, nothing like that. It's just a bit complicated, and she doesn't live near me anymore. But it's okay because I have you now, and Daddy, so what more could I want?"

"That's true, Mummy. You're very lucky!"

"Well, why don't you show me how lucky I am by setting the table after you're done?

Josie set about her job with pride, just as she knew her father would like to see her when he returned home.

Michael was approaching his forties when Josie arrived and made him a father. Even at such an age, he hadn't lost control of anything, his own body included. Everything was still in order. He was the kind of man women still noticed, and Sylvie was no exception. And the way in which he took to fatherhood made him the apparently perfect package.

During the first year of parenting, with its cocktail of relief, exhaustion, and — sometimes — loneliness, he had been their saviour, their knight in shining armour, welcomed as soon as he stepped through the door. At first, he made them both feel like royalty. They were his princesses.

"We are a proper family now," Michael would say. "No one can touch us and we couldn't be happier."

It was more of a statement than a suggestion; one of the many that almost had a hypnotic effect on Sylvie.

It's still worth it. I regret nothing.

The words filled her head as she watched him pull up in the driveway just after 6 pm, parking his new car proudly outside their impressive house. It was the kind of home Sylvie once drove past, imagining lives of splendour and comfort lived inside. For her own destiny, she had pictured owning a French deli on some street corner. But for now, she was free to take care of her family after putting her dreams on hold and closing off from everyone.

She still clung to how Michael made her feel in the early days when she was consumed by the reassurance of his presence. Physically, he was everything a man should be. He was also soft-spoken and never took his eyes off her when she talked, lavishing her with attention, flattery, and devotion. According to him, Sylvie was the most beautiful thing in his life, and that was something she chose—needed—to believe in. Sylvie had learned from her mother that it was all right to rely on another adult.

It didn't take long for the truth to rise to the surface, though. Josie was three the first time she realised that something was off.

"I've found a great nursery. It's just up the road, and the staff seemed so wonderful."

Michael was shifting about the kitchen, measuring the ingredients for his protein milkshake. He needed to drink it every morning at eight-fifteen sharp, as per his schedule. There was no deviation from it, and also no reaction to her words, so Sylvie kept talking.

"They have this beautiful outdoor space, with a miniature forest and seats made of tree stumps. It's perfect, Josie will love it. And the other children seemed so happy and content."

"I don't understand why you would want someone else to look after our child," she said. Those words cut through Sylvie like a knife. "You are not working, anyway. What are you going to do with your time if you are not with Josie?"

"It's three mornings a week, Michael. Can't you see it would be good for both of us to be allowed to miss each other a bit?"

"There will be plenty of time for that when she goes to school, surely?"

Shortly after Josie turned seven, Sylvie tried again to test the water with Michael about pursuing a life outside the home, but his ice-cold response killed her confidence a little more each time.

Sylvie had planned to attend a professional cookery school, but she gave up trying to find a way to tell him. He wouldn't approve. Instead, she busied herself with looking after family, keeping her daughter close by to comfort her, but Josie remained a little bit in awe of her father still.

"Did you know that a bunch of peas has more *poteen* than an egg, Daddy?"

"More—? Oh, I think you mean protein, Josie," he said, in a tone that was a bit patronising. It was lost on his daughter, but not his wife.

"Daddy, I don't know who puts the peas inside the pods when they are growing. Do you?"

"I'm not sure. Maybe your Mummy knows? Or maybe someone could feed me before I get any more questions?"

He crossed the room and put a firm hand on Sylvie's waist. It felt a bit too firm, but she still rewarded him with a smile. A well-rehearsed one. Then, she turned her attention back to their meal, knowing it needed to be served on the fine China.

"Doesn't Mummy look pretty tonight, Josie? She knows that's my favourite dress."

"Yes, Daddy, she's prettier than Ballet Barbie!"

They ate in an air of stilted calm. Sylvie found some peace in the chance to sit back and watch them eat the meals she prepared. Before long, her husband looked at his watch in an exaggerated fashion.

"Oh dear, I believe you should be in the bath by now. Do you have any progress to show me on that reward chart we've been working on?"

Sylvie watched as their daughter cowered slightly at her father's expectant tone and disappeared upstairs quickly.

"I'll be up shortly to run your bath, my darling."

Sylvie continued to pick at her food while her husband watched her. She had only had a slice of toast and two strong coffees throughout the day. Michael cast his eye around, from the vast kitchen to the utility room, where clothes formed an abandoned pile. It was going to be a tough evening, but Michael looked ready to take control like he always did.

"Have you been a bit distracted today, my love? Not like you to leave the laundry out."

She shrank on herself a little, ashamed.

"Not to worry, perhaps you have some of your award-winning cheesecake hidden in the back of the fridge today?" he asked, his tone urgent. Sylvie could feel him pulling her out of her own head, as he knew he couldn't reach her there. But she wanted to hide for a little longer.

"There's cheesecake in the fridge, yes. I think I will run Josie's bath and jump in one afterward myself, if you don't mind, darling?"

Michael's eyes were on her as she poured herself a glass of Chablis, before disappearing upstairs. Soon, the smell of lavender drifted through the house.

Once the door was locked, Sylvie let herself sink into the bathtub, reaching out only to sip some wine. Little by little, her gaze drifted to the cupboard above the sink, where she stashed her pills. She just wanted to float away, to a place where there was no shame or sadness.

Not again, Sylvie. Not again.

As she let her mind wander, she recalled her daughter's words. *Sisters who live together forever.*

If only she knew.

Chapter 15

SYLVIE

Glasgow 2007

Waking early on the morning of her wedding anniversary, Sylvie's first thought was the same as every other day — please let today be a good one. She knew that Michael would have something special planned and needed the day to go well. She walked slowly to her dressing room, with her head still full of mist. Michael must have put her to bed last night, at least judging by the buttons of her silk pajamas; she'd been too inebriated to get them right.

The red linen shift dress waited for her, hanging from her wardrobe. His choice again; he told Sylvie it reminded him of their first date. Part of her wanted to put on the jeans and sweatshirt she hid in the back, but he was watching her, standing by the door with a coffee in his hand.

The jeans will have to wait, she thought.

Michael walked calmly towards her, placing a mug of something hot on her bedside table. He was very thoughtful that way, thought Sylvie. Seems to know how to help, before she knew herself.

"Strong with a splash of cream — just what you need, Sylvie."

Need, not *want.* Michael always chose his words with care.

"Hope you're remembering it's our special day today?"

Michael was never overtly critical, but the subtle aftershock of his words always struck Sylvie with a final sting. At first, she dismissed this as paranoia in her own head.

"It is, darling. A very special day. I just need to wake up a little. Has Josie had her breakfast?"

"Yes. An hour ago. She's been waiting for Mummy to join us."

Shame returned to her in spades. She avoided his gaze and headed towards the shower, her coffee in hand. Around half an hour later, Sylvie joined her family in the lounge, where Michael welcomed her arrival with a rather grand sweeping of his arm.

"Here's Mummy now, Josie. I told you she was on her way down. She's even put on my favourite dress — how perfect."

"Happy Anniversary Mummy! I made you a card."

"Oh, my darling! What a gorgeous girl you are, Josie Miller. Please tell me all about these flowers and this garden. Is it our garden?"

"Yes, Mummy! These are your bluebells and here I am sitting next to you. I gave us a bench to sit on just in case you were having a tired day."

Sylvie's heart felt like it might burst with love.

"Could we all go for a walk this morning and have a picnic? Do you think you're up to organising that?"

She was sure that Michael's thinly veiled patronising tone was noticed, but only by her.

#

The park was busy. Children packed into the play area, families lingering around the pond and feeding the ducks next to signs telling them not to.

The Miller family was led to a quiet corner near the woods. Michael liked to have a buffer between his world and other people's, and he told his family as much. Why would they want to be among the madness when they had everything they needed already? Their own spot, their own company.

"No one loves you like Daddy does," he said as they huddled together and ate out of their grand picnic box, on expensive picnic plates.

In the distance, the other children chased each other and asked for slush puppies from the Mr   Whippy van. It felt like they were watching a movie, Sylvie thought.

"Sylvie!"

A high-pitched shriek pierced their bubble.

"Sylvie! Look, Chloe, it's Josie from school!"

One of Josie's classmates and her mum had spotted them. Next to her, Michael tensed up while Josie began waving at the sight of a familiar face. Sylvie had less than five seconds to remember the name of the woman who was striding towards them like Sylvie was a long-lost friend.

Meg.

"Well, we've just arrived and were heading to the play park to take our chances with the rabble," Meg said. Just like her daughter, she was full of confidence. "Fancy joining us?"

"Can we go too, Mum, can we? Please!"

Sylvie looked at Michael. It was an involuntary yet automatic reflex.

"Have you met my husband, Meg? Michael, this is Meg. Chloe is in Josie's cl—"

"We've met before, I believe. Lovely to see you again, Meg."

Sylvie winced at the sharpness of his tone.

"Daddy, can we sit with Chloe's family?" Josie asked.

"I'm sorry, darling, but we have to go in a minute."

Catherine's crestfallen face prompted Sylvie to speak up without checking her words first. "Do we?"

Michael just stared at her, silent and waiting.

Sylvie moved quickly to make an awkward gesture of self-reprimanding, knocking her hand against her own forehead. Her husband continued to avoid eye contact with both women.

"Gosh, Meg, sorry—my mistake—yes, we have this thing to do this afternoon. I totally forgot. Michael, I mean, Josie has an appointment about... oh, it's a shoe fitting. School shoes, so best not to cancel. You know how booked up they get. Maybe we will bump into you again soon. We're often in the park on a Saturday afternoon."

The awkwardness was not lost on either of them, but Meg steered Chloe away, regardless. "No worries, Sylvie! I'll leave you to your, eh, shoe thing? Come on, Chloe! Next time, sweetheart."

Josie's face crumbled, while Chloe seemed to recover from the rejection right away and bounced off after her mother. The moment they were out of earshot, Michael started complaining.

"Why must we make up excuses just to spend time as a family?"

"I wasn't... I just didn't want to be rude, Michael."

"And is it not rude to abandon your husband to hang out with strangers?"

"They're not strangers. I see Meg on most days, along with many other parents. It's my only opportunity for conversation."

Visibly affronted by the challenge to his own beliefs, Michael rose and zipped up his hooded jacket, and waited for the others to follow suit.

"Come on, Josie, I think it's time to head home. Mummy is bored with us already."

Sylvie endured the both of them sulking for the rest of the day. It made her think twice about talking to a school friend when they were at the park.

Chapter 16

SYLVIE

Glasgow 2007

The day after their visit to the park, Michael stopped sulking after some fawning from Sylvie's part. He believed he got his point across; she knew it, and she didn't speak as she watched him eat his poached eggs.

"Perhaps you could make use of the home gym you wanted so much when Josie's at school. Those extra pounds won't shift themselves."

When he leant over to kiss her forehead, Sylvie flinched. She knew he must have felt it, but chose to just hover a little longer over her in response.

Michael picked up the keys of his black Range Rover, the status symbol she hated the most. It reminded her of a gangster's car, and she felt uncomfortable sitting in it. But mostly, she was aware of a growing relief the moment he left the house. It was hard to describe why, but it was there, washing over her, gently, nonetheless. Her eyes followed him as he left for work; once there, he'd be the all-conquering hero of his own world, surrounded by colleagues who jumped when he called.

Sylvie faced yet another colourless day instead, with the usual rounds of school runs, housework, and long walks around the neighbourhood. Her boundaries were set by trimmed hedges and a gated community.

She tried so hard to fight the inevitable moments of darkness that swept over her mind,   each one pushing her back to that place of fear, self-loathing, and abandonment. No matter how hard she tried to distract herself, her life was too empty to avoid the painful questions. Why had she ended up feeling so alone? Even with her longed-for daughter by her side and a man who could provide every material comfort she could want. Still, when the emptiness stretched out in front of her for the next five hours, she had to fight back the dark thoughts.

It wasn't your fault. None of this. You are not the one who changed the plan.

Thoughts of Ava and the life she would be living flooded her head with a constant gnawing sensation. They were painful enough, but then she thought of Josie, and then Catherine, and the pain was almost unbearable. She had so many unanswered questions.

Sylvie drifted into daydreams of seeing them again and of Josie smiling with the adventure of it all. But she knew there was no route to this moment that wouldn't be blocked by him. Michael had them where he wanted, and this time, no one was coming to rescue her. She reached for her mobile phone, but it wasn't there. Odd. she could have sworn she left it there.

I really am losing my mind, she thought as she opened the pill box on the section marked 'MON' and dutifully took her day's allocation. Michael had set out her week's pills   last night, as he always did on a Sunday. He kept them locked away in a cupboard, to protect Sylvie from any accidental mistakes with dosage, as he called it. He didn't know about her secret stash in the bathroom cupboard, hidden in a box of waxing products. He'd never look there, and she needed to have her little secrets, too.

As she stared out of her window, she imagined the city waking up: coffee machines would start up and coffee would brew, busy kitchens would chop vegetables for their patrons. Stories would be shared, problems discussed, and business plans would be made. Life would burst while she sat in her gilded tower, with nothing but daytime television and her ironing board to keep her company.

The days when Sylvie secretly planned her new career at the helm of a deli and restaurant in the heart of Glasgow's bustling West End seemed nothing more than a faded memory now.

Chapter 17

AVA

Edinburgh, 2007

Almost four long months after Ava sent the letter to Sylvie, she resigned herself to the fact that no reply was coming.
"Let it go, Ava," said Sean, who was losing his own belief with every passing day.
"It's not the right time. We just have to move on, at least for now   ."
"Sean, it's not like I'm waiting for the first signs of summer. It's Catherine's life. It's our life."

"Do you think I don't know that?" He raised his eyebrows in one swift move that should silence Ava's painful protests, but she was impervious.

"Sometimes I wonder, Sean. You seem to find it easier to discard emotions than I do."

Ava regretted her words at once, but she had said them now. That's the painful thing about words, she thought. There's no return policy if she chose them badly or they don't quite fit.

He seemed to recover well, even if, for the first time, she could see true pain in his eyes. What was he trying to tell her? "Is that how it looks, Ava? Really?

You told me you would wait until everyone was ready before even considering this. She is clearly telling you she's not, and you... *we* need to respect that."

"She is telling me nothing! That's just not the same thing."

For all his patience, Sean had a breaking point, and Ava could sense when she had reached it. She fell silent.

"I've got to go, Ava. I've got a job this weekend and I need to get on the road."

"Leaving me again? Where's this one, then?"

"It's in Dundee. I've got to be on site for two full days. Early starts, long days, and a soulless hotel room waiting for me. All very glamorous and clandestine. "

Her heart sank.

They used to look forward to their weekends together, as they meant family teatime with Catherine and the evening spent on the sofa. It was the time where they could just be husband and wife, not parents or people with commitments and responsibilities. Now the thought of a quiet night at the hotel seemed strangely preferable, at least to Sean. He had to work — she knew that, and she knew that weekends were often the busiest. Ava was also aware that her husband loved some female company. Could he have found comfort in someone else?

Stop it now. This isn't helping.

#

Ava arrived at school with a minute to spare. She watched from her chosen spot as other parents chatted among themselves. Ava was never comfortable with that type of small talk, and she tended to avoid it. At any rate, Catherine soon came running towards her.

"Hello you! Have you had a good day, honey?"

Catherine gripped her mum tightly around the waist in a way that felt like a release of something heavy — relief, perhaps.

"Sorry to bother you," Mrs Reid said. She was Catherine's teacher and always spoke in soft tones. "Do you have a minute?"

A shiver went down Ava's spine, but Mrs Reid picked it up at once.

"Don't worry, Mrs Peterson, please. It's just that I wondered if you had a few minutes to chat. Preferably on the phone?"

"Phone? Erm, yes, of course. Has something happened? Is Catherine okay?"

"She's such an able pupil. A joy to have in the class. I only wanted to touch base on some other areas; we like to chat with the parents from time to time."

Ava had no idea what it meant, as she didn't have the tools to translate teacher-speak.

"Is everything okay, Mummy?" Catherine was still waiting for her. "What did Mrs Reid say to you? I've done all my homework on time this week, I promise. Did she say I was talking in class? It wasn't me, Mum. It was the other girls. It just looked like it was me because—"

"Oh, calm down, honey. You're not in trouble. I think your teacher just likes to share progress with the parents every now and again. It will be lovely to hear a bit more about school! Now, let's get home before we get locked in the playground."

Catherine's routine after school rarely deviated from its usual schedule. She would throw her bag down, grab a snack, and run to her room. Ava felt she needed this sound to anchor herself back to the familiarity of home. She would emerge after about an hour, looking for company and dinner before settling down to read a book. She loved her books, and she loved imagining the worlds that they transported her to in her mind.

Ava was desperate for Sean to come home that night. Much as she hated to admit it, she needed him to be a parent and a husband; to listen, support, and make her feel a little less alone.

Ava also enjoyed her evening routine. The sequence of dinner, bath and reading was a leveler in her life, too. Like mother, like daughter, as the saying goes.

"Goodnight, my angel. Mummy loves you more than chocolate, you know that, don't you?"

"That's a lot of love, Mummy!"

Less than an hour later, Ava was wrapped in the comfort of her own sheets, relishing the peace and quiet of a moment devoid of urgent need from another human. She fell asleep almost at once and woke up in almost the very same position.

#

Mrs Reid called the next day at six o'clock.

"Hello, Mrs Peterson, how are you?"

Mrs Reid had a soft, lilting tone — no doubt developed over many years in the classroom. It felt reassuring, yet firm.

"Yes, okay… I mean, is everything okay with Catherine?"

"Like I said, Catherine is a delightful student. She takes her learning very seriously, and I'm pleased with her progress."

Ava could feel a *but* rising to the surface. "I just wondered if she ever draws or paints for you at home?"

"Pardon?"

Images came flooding back to her, through the overloaded mess of her own mind. The pictures she and Sean had poured over at home. She had blocked them out of her mind as she tried to cope with Sylvie's silence. But she remembered them only too well. The reflection of a mind in turmoil. Her own daughter. Trying to express something through her art that she couldn't put into words. Ava had hoped that this would be a private darkness that she could contain and manage at home. But now it was staring her in the face from outside her front door.

"I know she draws a lot, yes, and my husband have seen a lot of her work at home. I know it can look a bit sad, sometimes, but — is there something I need to know?"

"I just thought I should mention that Catherine often spends her break and lunchtime in the classroom. You know, just drawing by herself. It's not a problem, Mrs Peterson. She's very easy company for me, but, well…"

"Is she not playing with her friends?"

"No, not very often. I get the impression that she would rather be in the classroom."

Ava knew that Catherine was having problems making friends, but the thought of her sitting on her own while the other kids were outside having fun was too much to bear.

"Is it not your job to do something about this? Encourage her to join in? How am I supposed to help when I'm not there?"

"Mrs Peterson, please, don't think—"

"How long has this been going on for?"

"Mrs Peterson, there's something else. It's her pictures. They are, sometimes, a bit… well… concerning."

For someone whose job is teaching others to communicate, she's making a poor job of getting to the point.

"What do you mean, *concerning*?"

"They seem to be getting, well, darker. There are monsters and sometimes blood. They seem to be a channel for something that is troubling her. That's the only way I can describe them. As I said, I didn't want to worry you. We just like to keep parents fully informed about anything they might want to discuss with their child. If you came into the classroom sometime, I could show you what I mean," Mrs Reid said. "Perhaps it's just a phase and Catherine will outgrow it when she learns to express herself in different ways. She's very talented, you know. I wish I could draw as well as she can!"

Ava could sense that Mrs Reid was trying to lift the mood, but it was too late. The damage was done, and she had already progressed to full panic with a side of shame.

"Thank you, Mrs Reid. I really appreciate your call."

As soon as the call ended, Ava rushed back to her daughter's bedside table and pulled open the drawers, which were crammed full of bits of paper. She lifted each piece at a time and laid them in front of her on the floor. The more she looked, the more she found.

Within minutes, Ava had covered Catherine's carpet with her child's work. There was no escaping it now. She realised that what she and Sean had found some months ago was just the tip of the iceberg, Ava laid out each image around her, not knowing where to look first. Just as before, the colours struck her first. All dark shades; so little light seemed to penetrate Catherine's world. And like a recurring dream, Catherine's drawings featured herself and another child. A haunting image that looked like a slightly different version of herself. In the picture, but always just somewhere in the background. *Catherine, my sweetheart. Who is this?* thought Ava, terrified of the answer to her own question.

And then she found the monsters. Ghoulish looking with mouths open and sharp teeth on show. Some bared mouths dripping with blood.

At once Ava imagined a similar pile of images being drawn or painted in that empty classroom at lunchtime. Ava's thoughts drifted further to her own childhood and the familiar comfort of her soulmate. The friend that was always just there. Not in dark shades of pastel on a piece of paper in a drawer, but for real. Tangible.

That was the moment she knew she needed to contact Sylvie more than ever. This time, she didn't overthink it. A little more basic research months ago and she had found out exactly where Sylvie lived in Glasgow.

All I want is to start talking again. She craved being able to sit down with her friend and just talk over a cup of coffee. She felt that would hurt no one. Knowing she could get to Glasgow and back in time to pick Catherine up from school, she longed for the days when the two girls used to share everything. Ava could not conceive of her best friend in the world closing the door to her. She knew the thing that bound them together for life could also be the thing that kept them apart.

"When's Daddy coming home?" Catherine asked, peppering her with anxious questions as they drove to school the next day.

"Daddy will be back in two sleeps, angel. I bet he misses you loads already!" Ava said. She feared it was not a good moment to drop her plans on Catherine, but she had no choice. "Mummy has to take a small trip today. I'll be back to pick you up at three o'clock, I promise. But, just in case I get stuck in traffic, I've asked Rebecca's mum to stay with you until I'm back. Okay, sweetie?"

Ava could see the tension building further in her daughter's face. She guessed that there was a nervousness about her being back in time to pick her up from school. Pulling up to their usual parking spot as close to the school gates as she could manage, Ava switched the engine off and turned towards her daughter.

"Don't worry, Catherine. I will drive safely, and I'll bring you a treat. Now, please, go to your classroom and have a happy day. I'll hear all about it tonight."

"I love you, Mummy."

Catherine gave her a brave yet shaky cuddle before jumping out of the car and going through the school gates. Tears had been welling up in her eyes and Ava did not know what scared her the most, the day ahead or that Ava might not be there to pick her up.

I love you too, baby.

At times, the terror of any harm that may come to Catherine paralysed Ava. She was the most precious thing in the world, Ava's sense of purpose, and all that felt overwhelming.

Chapter 18

AVA

Glasgow, 2007

Ava pulled up outside Sylvie's place around half past ten. She knew Michael was now a wealthy man, but she wasn't prepared for such opulence. The wide gravel path leading to an immense Victorian building had pillars guarding the gates, and the house itself had more windows and chimneys than all the houses on Ava's street combined. The landscaped garden had a trampoline installed, so big she could see the top of it from over the hedge.

Cameras followed her as she walked towards the front door. It had a brass door-knocker, and Ava tried to imagine it at Christmas, with some elaborate hand-woven wreath hanging from it.

Everything felt alien, so far removed from her flat in Stockbridge. In Ava's world, just one false move or one unforeseen major expense and stress levels could escalate uncontrollably.

Her eyes darted all around while she pressed on the doorbell; the garage doors were closed, offering no clues. Maybe Sylvie wasn't home.

Oh God, I've come this far, and it's all for nothing. What is wrong with you, you mad woman?

Then she heard keys rustling on the other side of the door. Once it swung open, Ava wondered if it was possible for someone to look familiar and a stranger at the same time. Sylvie had the same eyes, nose, and mouth Ava remembered; a few more lines on her face, too, but that was that. Gone was the carefree friend of Ava's youth. In her place, there was a shadow of the woman she expected to see.

"Ava?"

Hearing Sylvie say her name felt to Ava like being transported back in time, where she could escape from her parents' cold hearts, their absence. Back then, Sylvie's company had been the one constant in her life. But here, after so many years, she felt like an intruder and shrank a little as Sylvie opened the door.

"Sylvie, it's me. I'm so sorry to just, you know, land on your doorstep."

Silence. No response. Zero. There was no reaction at all from the friend she hadn't seen in seven years.

"Sylvie?"

"...Ava?"

Oh, thank God, Ava thought, looking at the figure in front of her. Sylvie seemed uncomfortable as she stood on her enormous porch. It made her look smaller and more vulnerable than Ava remembered.

"Can I come in?"

"I — was just… yes, of course, Ava. Michael isn't here now, but he'll be back soon."

That struck Ava as an odd thing to say since she hadn't been asking after Michael.

It's not him I've missed, you know.

She was here to see her friend, and that's all. Well, almost all. It was step one.

Their first few moments together felt awkward. The house was quiet, eerily so, and there was no evidence of a young child living there. In her world, homes were full of abandoned boots or dirty clothes, Lego, and assorted plastic crap.

Oh God, what's happened to Josie? Ava thought as they made their way to the kitchen. *A child cannot live in this house. It's like an untouched show home.*

"Ava, I can't believe you're here. I mean, I'm sorry. If you'd warned me, I would have…" Sylvie said, then her voice trailed into nothing.

Would have what? I wasn't expecting a red carpet. Where's Josie?

"Sorry. I didn't have your number."

"I was just preparing some coffee. Would you like some?"

"…Josie! Where is Josie?" Ava's voice had an uncontrollable edge of desperation.

"She's at school, Ava."

Shit, of course. School. Where your own daughter is, too.

"Sorry, your house is just so—" Sylvie looked as if she knew her thoughts, and bowed her head. "—A coffee would be great, thanks."

Their past friendship was not marked by coffee, but by teeth-rotting sodas, cocktails, and Pinot Grigio. Now, Sylvie dressed in expensive cashmere and linen loungewear, using a coffee machine that looked more expensive than Ava's car.

"Josie's at school, you said?"

"She is, yes. It's such a surprise to see you, Ava. How did you know we were…"

"You were what?"

"Never mind, it's just… I'm so glad you're here. How did you find me?"

I can't tell her the truth. I can't tell her I hunted her down by researching her husband like a private detective, then tricking a colleague into giving me his address.

"Just, you know, using my unique talent for nosiness. Oh, and it's a hard house to miss, this one, and many people know who's just moved in. Michael's in the news! Regular legal hero, by all accounts."

A blank, distant smile met Ava's feeble attempts at humour. Still, Ava plowed on, determined to fill the gaping hole between them.

"You just left the country, Sylvie. After everything we agreed on."

"I know, and I'm so sorry. But, it wasn't my—I mean, Michael thought it was for the best—"

"Did you get my letter, Sylvie?"

Sylvie's face immediately jumped from shame to something different.

"Why didn't you reply? I'm sorry for tracking you down like that, but I thought we agreed we would always listen when one of us wanted to chat about, you know, the future."

Sylvie carefully placed the fine bone china cup on the table and looked straight at Ava.

"I didn't get a letter, Ava."

Ava smarted, feeling a rising disbelief expand in her own head.

"I sent it two months ago. To this address. Michael's secretary gave it to me."

Ava could tell from her face that Sylvie was totally in the dark about the existence or contents of the letter.

"What was in it?"

There was a look of genuine fear and nervousness on Sylvie's face, and Ava did not know what she wanted to hear. So, she went with the truth.

"What do you think it said? I was asking to meet you. Catherine is growing up so fast and asking so many questions and, I know you may not feel the same, but I just wanted to talk to you about, well, getting together. That's all."

"That's all? That's quite a lot, Ava."

"I just miss having you in my life. And, well, it's Catherine. She gets lonely sometimes."

There was no turning back now. Ava knew Sylvie had only said a handful of words so far, most of them about coffee, so she stopped talking and waited.

"Why now?" Sylvie asked in the end. Two more words.

"I almost had an accident, you see. A car accident. It could have been nasty, but I'm fine, but—it could have ended in a different way, and if I was no longer here... Sylvie, the girls deserve to meet. Or, at least, we deserve to think about it, you know, properly. Together."

Stop talking, for God's sake.

Sylvie would have to fill the silence and tell her it was too soon. The girls were too young. It was too much to cope with. None of that came, though. Sylvie just stood there and listened until Ava ran out of steam.

"Say something, please."

"I... I just wasn't prepared for this. Here. Today."

"I know, and I'm sorry. I don't know why the letter didn't arrive. I should have sent another before just pitching up on your doorstep, but I was afraid I would talk myself out of it. But then, I just kept thinking, what harm would it do? Even once, to see how it goes. For all of us, that is."

"I've often thought about this moment. Ava. The day when the past catches up with us."

"You say that like it's a bad thing."

"No, no, sorry, I didn't mean that. I'm just—well, if I'm honest, I'm just scared."

Ava was scared too, but Sylvie's fear seemed somehow different. She was constantly looking out of the window or checking her watch, and Ava wondered about her life, about whichever events had changed her. Was Sylvie still the person who promised to raise her daughter together with Ava's? She opened her mouth to throw Sylvie an escape rope, but Sylvie beat her to it.

"Okay. Okay, let's talk about this properly, but not today. Not now."

There it was. Just for a moment. The sparkle in her eyes that Ava remembered seeing when life tempted her with something so delicious that she couldn't hide her own emotions. It was there when Michael asked her to dance at the end-of-term party. It was there when she showed Ava her Mum's jewellery box bursting with bracelets, necklaces, and earrings that they would both dream of wearing one day. This time the temptation Ava offered was more than the charms of any handsome young boy and glittered more than the sparkle of any jewel. The stakes were higher. It was Sylvie's chance to reconnect with her dearest friend in the world and watch as they reintroduced the girls who were born seconds apart seven years ago.

The old spark Ava knew so well spread across Sylvie's face. An instant later, it was already gone.

"I have to speak to Michael, though. I have to speak to my husband."

Michael again. The man who apparently wielded power over everything.

Is that what happens in other marriages? Is the dutiful wife bowing to her husband? No, I'm being unfair, Ava. He's Josie's father now, and this is a big deal. He deserves to have a say.

"I have to go now, but please, promise me you'll think about it."

Sensing that she was close to overstaying her welcome, Ava gathered her coat and checked her watch   before heading back to her car. As she was leaving, a now visibly anxious Sylvie began to scribble something on a note, before passing it to Ava, holding on to her hand for a moment as she did so. *Don't be late Mum, please.*

She could hear Catherine's pleas echoing in her head.

Ava drove back to Edinburgh while a million emotions went through her mind. Guilt, excitement, panic, they were all accounted for when she navigated along Scotland's busiest stretch of motorway. Then, panic won as she saw an enormous queue of cars approaching the capital.

"Shit. Not today. Please. May the traffic jam gods shine on me right now."

Her mind flooded with thoughts of Catherine searching for her among the crowd of other parents, and she glared at the car in front of her. Maybe sheer will would be enough to clear the way? The aging clutch groaned with the strain first gear was putting on it, but she still made it back in time.

"Mum!"

Catherine hadn't mastered the art of looking disinterested at seeing her yet, and gave Ava a warm smile and a powerful hug.

"I told you I'd be here, sweetheart. Now, how was your day?"

#

After shutting the door of her daughter's bedroom, Ava tiptoed back downstairs.

She had three deadlines looming and Sean wouldn't be home soon, but she felt too spent by the day's events to think about that. Somehow, she had to process everything.

If in doubt, do your research.

It was a piece of advice Ava got from her tutor at the University and she stuck to it to this day. She poured herself a glass of Gin Tonic and then she began researching the husband of her former best friend. It felt rational. It felt justified. But mostly, she just couldn't stop herself.

She started with a simple Google search. She didn't have much to go on but started with what she did know.

First search: *Michael Miller, Lawyer, Glasgow.*

Ava knew nothing about Sylvie's husband, except what she remembered from their childhood. She never trusted him then. Each time she felt his eyes on her in the school playground felt intrusive. She had just turned sixteen, he was working as an apprentice at a local car dealership — saving money for university — and he made her skin crawl. He would wander around the school playground at lunchtime, waiting for the older girls to walk out to the local sandwich shop or KFC for their lunch. There was something in the way he hovered around them that made her want to scream. She was almost always with Sylvie and secretly hoped it was her he was after. Then, one day, when she was alone, he cornered her outside the school gates when no one was looking.

"What's wrong, Ava? Looking a bit glum today, heh? Reckon you need an older boyfriend to show you what life's all about!"

"Go away, Michael. I'm not interested."

"What's wrong? Think you're better than me, Ava? Doubt that - I know your Mum is a drunk and your dad did a runner on her years ago. Think you'd be grateful for some male attention, don't you?"

"Piss…off!"

When he eventually got the message, Ava felt the briefest of victories until he put the final knife in her back by turning his attention to Sylvie.

I should have warned you properly then, Sylvie. I should've made you believe me about him.

Sylvie and Michael had married in their early twenties and his control over their lives tightened with every passing year. Ava and Sylvie had promised each other repeatedly that they would stay close until the day the girls could learn the truth, but Michael had other ideas and Ava had no contact with her since they left the country only a month after Josie was adopted. Even the Christmas cards had stopped coming, but she never stopped thinking about her best friend.

Returning to the search results on the screen in front of her, she could see that the fruits of her labour were so far deadly dull.

'Michael Miller on Dispute Resolution in Corporate Mergers.'

'Michael Miller's perspective on life in the Legal 500 Fastlane.'

Give me strength —   does anyone have to actually read this stuff, thought Ava, close to abandoning her mission in favour of some Netflix light relief.

The boredom of wading through online legal articles that Michael Miller had given his name to was almost enough to tempt Ava to cut short her detective mission. But then one specific, unavoidable, and sickening headline caught her eye:

'Wealthy Glasgow lawyer cleared of historic sexual abuse allegations: Michael Miller vows to rebuild his shattered life and reputation but claims to hold no grudge against his false accusers.'

Ava felt bile rise from the pit of her stomach.

There was no photo attached. She knew it could have been him. Must have been. Glasgow is a relatively small place and everything about this felt like it must be him. *Wow, that's what you call baggage, Sylvie.*

By now, Ava was one strong gin and tonic down and had achieved ninety percent of nothing worth an income. She had, however, wound herself up further about the events of the day and immersed herself in the apparent injustices inflicted on a man she had not even met.

By the time Sean strolled through the door, Ava was fighting the need to sleep and was ready to pounce.

"Another late one, I guess?" she asked. It was the most restrained comment she could manage, but her resentment shone through. "Working hard, are you?" he shot back.

"It's been a hell of a day, Sean, and I really wanted to talk to you. Why were you not answering any of my calls?"

"Well, for one thing, I've been back-to-back with client meetings, and then I had to prepare a new business pitch for tomorrow. I locked myself away where no one could find me, and the Wi-Fi was as strong as the coffee."

"Why have you always got a comeback for everything?"

"I have to keep up with you, my beloved. Got any more of that?" he said, pointing to Ava's G&T.

"I might, but it'll cost you. I need some serious, well-considered, and genuine conversation."

"That's nice. I hope you find it. What do you want with me, then?"

People would think Sean to be a bit of a smart arse. Ava knew there was more beneath the surface, instead, but he was good at hiding his feelings. She wondered how it was possible for them to love and drive each other to madness at the same time.

Ava knew she had to admit to Sean that she had visited Sylvie, and the words fell out of her mouth in an uncontrollable stream.

"I went to Glasgow today. To visit her. Well, both of them. But she was at school, of course. Josie, I mean. Sylvie was there though. She was so…   it was like she was scared…   oh God, what have I done, Sean?"

"Okay. Were you going to tell me about reaching this stage of *our* plan?"

"I think I did. You know, the other night?"

"And did it all pan out the way you imagined?"

"I'm not sure. She was so nervous at first, but then she seemed to relax very slightly, until…"

The beginning of Sean's *I told you so* expression was forming on his face.

"Don't look at me like that."

Ava lifted her right hand and spread her fingers out wide in rejection of Sean's cynicism.

"I don't know, it was weird. It was like her first instinct was to jump at the chance with open arms. Then she mentioned her husband, and she seemed to retreat. It was like a warning, that he might not be up for this as he's kind of protective, you know?

"I guess the man has a right to that."

"Yes, and I get that, Sean, but there was something else. She looked uncomfortable, almost afraid. And the other weird thing… she was a shadow of the woman I remember, so meek and thin. She just didn't look well."

"And at that point you thought, cracking time to introduce our daughter to this family, right?"

"Please lay off the sarcasm, Sean, something wasn't right. I know that woman better than I've known anyone else."

"You *knew* her, Ava. It's been seven years. Do I need to tell you how much people can change in seven years?"

"It doesn't matter. I'm going to visit her again soon."

Sean poured his drink in the kitchen before returning to his seat, swirling the ice cubes in his glass and swallowing at once. After rubbing the rough patch of stubble that had gathered around his jawline, he looked his wife straight in the eyes.

"Looks like you've made up your mind without my input, then?"

"Why won't you talk to me about this properly? Is there somewhere else you need to be?"

As the words came from her mouth, Ava could hear just how unreasonable she was being and tried to silence herself.

"Bed, Ava. Just bed."

His words didn't feel like an invitation to join him, and that hurt. She was tired, confused, but also knew she had to keep Sean on her side, though, at least if she wanted to make it in one piece.

"Oh, and the other thing—Catherine's teacher spoke to me today about her disturbing drawings. And I found the rest of them. All of them. We've got to talk to her about this. I don't know what's going on in her head, Sean."

"Let's just not jump to any dramatic conclusions yet, shall we? We will talk to her in a calm and rational way tomorrow."

For all her self-determinism and need for independence, Ava felt her whole body relax at the sound of the word *we*. She drove him to his limits, but was still deeply in love with this man and needed him to want her like he did when they first met. Scooping themselves out of the sofa, Ava and Sean abandoned the gin glasses where they sat and took each other's hand as they walked upstairs to bed. Ava switched the kitchen light off behind them and felt weak in her husband's warm hands, knowing that he still made her feel protected and loved as no one else could.

Chapter 19

AVA

Edinburgh, 2007

"Has anyone seen my work file?"

"Ava, I swear you lose at least one important item a day."

"Save the sarcasm, please. If you help me find it, there's a decent chance I will meet my deadline and get paid for this."

"Why don't you start here, then," he said, handing Ava her laptop briefcase from behind Catherine's sports bag.

Hunting for her notes in a slightly manic fashion, a folded piece of paper fell out at her feet.

In her haste to get home for Catherine, she had just got Sylvie's mobile number from her before racing to her car.

Now it was a bad time to think about this. Now was the time to deliver some work to her clients, pay the bills, and get her life in order. And so, she did what any reasonable woman in her position would do and reached for her phone.

This time, her words had to be light and powerful. She had taken the first step, but Sylvie had her own life now, and Michael — Michael had quite a firm hold on his family, Ava believed, and she knew that ignoring his presence would not be an option.

She tried not to overthink it and started typing.

-So lovely to see you, Sylvie. I'm sorry I came without warning. Please, can we do it again? I'm not angry that you pulled out of our agreement. I understand why, and I just want us to start again now. We can take this at your speed. Love, always, Ava. X-

Hard to ignore, to the point, and it wouldn't put too much pressure on Sylvie, she hoped.

A full day passed with no response, then a week, then three weeks.

"Why would she just ghost me again, Sean? This is too important."

"I don't know how you women think, Ava, but I'd hazard a guess. It is because it's too important, which is why she's taking her time to respond. You landed on her doorstep, after all."

"How can you be so patient about this?"

"That's a stupid question. We have no choice. We have our own family to focus on."

Frustration was mounting in Ava. She knew how much Sean loved Catherine, and that he would do anything to make her life complete; she knew it was irrational to expect more from him now, and yet she couldn't stop herself.

"This is your daughter's twin, you know! Or have you forgotten that?"

Too far. That had been cruel, and he didn't deserve it.

"That was a low blow, Ava," he said as he showed her his back and headed for the door. The ever-observant Catherine must have been alerted to the tension and appeared in the doorway.

"Mum? Dad? Is everything okay?"

Catherine.

Ava turned around. "Catherine. Yes, darling, everything is just fine. Are you ready for school? Let's walk today. I'd love to have a proper chat with you."

Pulling on their coats together, Ava felt lifted by the feel of fresh air on her face and the chance to talk to Catherine for some precious, uninterrupted moments before the day took over.

Ava knew it wouldn't be long before Catherine refused to let her m   um walk her to school or hug her in public.

Apparently, seven is a tricky age. Still young enough to need their parents so desperately on the tough days, but trying hard to find their own way in the world too.

She hoped she could unearth some clues about what was going on at school as well.   *That's what responsible parents do, isn't it? She thought. Keep it light, Ava, don't scare her off, though!*

"Are you enjoying school, sweetie?"

She ignored her mother and kept singing her favourite Disney tune.

"Catherine," Ava pressed on, "is there anything on your mind?"

"What do you mean, Mum?"

"I mean, anything at all. Anything in school that you're not happy with."

"Like what? I got four gold stars in my jotter last week. I showed you!"

"Oh, I know! You're such a clever girl! I guess I meant, leaving the learning bit aside. Are you making new friends?"

She looked at Ava and shrugged. Not an encouraging sign; it was a mirror image of her father's well-practiced move when he wanted to avoid a topic.

"Who would you like to have a playdate, or maybe a sleepover?"

"Mum, can we talk about something else?"

This was not a normal reaction for a seven-year-old to the prospect of a sleepover. As a lonely child herself, Ava had revelled at the chance to spend any time at Sylvie's home, watching movies, eating sweets, and talking until they couldn't hold their eyes open.

"What about Rebecca, sweetheart? She invited you to her party not so long ago. Would she like to come for a visit?"

"She told me she only invited me because her mum said she had to invite the whole class."

These words cut like a dagger through Ava's heart. *What spoilt little brat would say something like that to my child? To any child?* Still, Ava kept going.

"Is there anyone that you would, you know, like to—"

"Mum, I don't think I know how to make friends. It's just so scary to try to be like them all the time."

Ava wanted to hug her tight and reassure her, but they were at the school gates already, and she could feel Catherine's light grip on her hand melt away.

"Hi, Catherine!" A group of three girls was waving at her from a distance.

"Oh look, there are some friendly faces!"

"They're just pretending to be nice because you're watching." It hurt.

Rage built inside her as she walked home, and she composed another message for Sylvie.

-Sylvie, I know this is hard. Please don't think it's easy for me either. I've never been patient. You know that, and I would love to see you again. Just to talk. Nothing more, I promise. Call me. Ax -

Then she sat down and stared at her phone, like a hawk. Every so often she would open a client brief on her laptop screen, true, but she would just end up staring at it, mindlessly scrolling the cursor through the page. Ten minutes later, her phone lit up.

-Hi Ava, this is Michael. Sylvie's not available now, but I'll make sure she sees your message -

I'm sorry, what? You'll do what? Did I call someone else?

No, she had sent a message to Sylvie's own mobile, and Michael—she could not imagine Sean behaving that way, replying to a message on her phone, on her behalf. It felt wrong. Besides, why on earth would Sylvie need Michael to make sure of anything?

Are there messages he makes sure she doesn't see?

Had her first letter just 'vanished' in the post and was her text from three weeks mysteriously intercepted before it made it to Sylvie's eyes? Ava's burning suspicions made her more resolute than ever to see her friend again soon. Whether she invited her or not, she was going anyway. Sean saw her pacing through the kitchen, barking incoherently about their daughter's cry for help and the coercive behaviour of her best friend's husband.

"You need to calm down, Ava."

"No, I don't. I need to find out what the heck is going on, and what kind of husband thinks it's appropriate to screen her text messages."

"It's their life. Try to remember that. And it's hardly evidence of domestic abuse."

"At best, it's bloody creepy, Sean."

"So, you're just going to abandon us for the day?"

"Abandon? No. I'm letting my daughter and her father spend some quality time together while I visit a dear friend I'm worried about."

"And this is all about looking out for Sylvie, yes? Nothing to do with pursuing your own agenda?"

Ava knew he had just hit a raw nerve, and so did Sean. At any rate, it was too late to change her mind. "Just let me go. The sooner I'm back, the sooner we can spend time together as a family."

"Just remember that we are a happy family, whatever the outcome of this may be."

There was a bitter edge in his tone. Ava knew he was trying to be heard and had a tendency to be right about things. Yes, she had an agenda now and she would succeed.

"I've seen Catherine's drawings too, remember, Sean."

She punched the words out at him like bullets, leaving him to make sense of them alone.

Chapter 20

AVA

Glasgow, 2007

By the time Ava reached the driveway, she had considered every possible way their conversation could go. She had planned what to say if Sylvie was alone, if Josie was present, or if Michael was present as well. He would not deter her from making her own decisions.

Ava hadn't, of course, thought about what to do if no one was in.

What an idiot. She could be anywhere. They could have gone on holiday. I could have been having pancakes with Catherine and Sean, followed by a walk in the park.

Painful flashbacks to Catherine's drawings and her own near miss flooded her mind, and she felt overwhelmed with competing thoughts and panic. Then she saw Sylvie pull up into the driveway, the shine of her silver Mercedes bright enough to blind her for a moment. At first, Ava thought she was on her own; once Sylvie drove closer, though, she noticed the girl sitting in the backseat.

Josie's hair was tied back in a bun, like a ballerina, allowing Ava to see her happy young face. It was like looking at Catherine, in a way. Textbook non-identical twins. So similar and yet so different.

How could it be that seven years had already passed since she brought this perfect girl into the world? Delivered at the same time, almost, and now Josie stared at Ava like she was just a passing stranger. The consequences of her own impetuosity made her feel like her heart would explode, and she searched within herself for strength. She couldn't act as if Josie was her child.

Oh God, what am I doing?

Anything she meant to say vanished from her mind. She had never felt so vulnerable in a very long time. But now she was exposed. Facing her friend, who was clearly thrown back into a state of pain.

"Hi Ava. Were we, um, expecting you?"

"No, no, you probably weren't," she said. "I'm sorry. I sent you a message—two, in fact. Michael said he would pass them on?"

Sylvie kept her head down, refusing to make eye contact. Ava was aware it was another uninvited visit but still felt affronted by the chill in the air.

"Josie, sweetheart," Sylvie said, fumbling with her keys to open the front door. "Could you take this bag to the kitchen? Mummy will catch up."

"Who's this, Mummy?"

Ava held back her instinct to speak. She and Sylvie looked at each other, vulnerable for a moment because of an innocent question.

"This is Mummy's friend, Josie. Her name is Ava."

"Ava? The one you were telling me about that time in the kitchen?" Josie asked, and Ava's heart danced a little.

"That's right, sweetheart."

"You're right, Mummy. She is very pretty."

With that, Sylvie pushed the heavy door open and pressed a fob against the security box before gently encouraging Josie inside. Ava was left standing outside, awkward and unsure whether to follow them.

"God, Sylvie, I'm so sorry. I just had to see you again, and she's, she's just perfect. Josie is just, so... I had to —"

"I know Ava. I know."

"Did you get my messages?"

"No, I think Michael might have deleted them by mistake. He's not great with technology."

Still a dreadful liar. In a way, Ava felt comforted by it; some things never changed

"Can I come in?"

"Sure..." Sylvie glanced at her watch and seemed to hesitate. "Michael will be home soon, though, and I'm not sure he —"

"I get it. He's not keen. That's okay, I understand, but he's not here now, is he? He's hardly going to burst in and call the police, right?"

Would he?

By now, both women and Josie were assembled in the kitchen, and Sylvie was attempting to busy herself putting away groceries in what looked like a walk-in larder in the corner of the room. Ava felt like she'd entered the set of some celebrity kitchen. Every shelf was arranged without an item of Tupperware out of place.

"Mummy, does your friend want some of the cake we made this morning?"

"I don't know, Josie, why don't you ask her?"

"Excuse me, Ava, would you like some cake?"

That was her chance, and she would not waste it. A warm smile appeared on Ava's face as she approached the little girl; Josie's eyes looked like Catherine's, but she had an air of self-confidence that Catherine seldom displayed.

"Josie, is it?" She nodded. "I would love some cake. Thank you."

Sylvie seemed to soften around the edges as she poured tea for everyone, and the three of them sat around the table, nibbling cake with silver forks. Watching Josie while she acted like a grownup reminded Ava of that scene in *Titanic*, where wealthy girls had tea together. Oh, how Catherine would giggle at this, Ava thought; she was doubtful her daughter had ever eaten cake with a fork.

"Do you bake a lot, Josie?" A bland question, but it didn't matter.

"Mummy and I bake and cook lots. Daddy likes it when we make him something fresh for dinner or for a weekend brunch."

I bet he does. Do you serve him when he rings the bell, wearing aprons and all?

"Josie, why don't you go and tidy up your room? Daddy will be home soon."

With the buffer that was Josie gone, they could no longer pretend everything was well. Surprisingly enough, Sylvie took the lead.

"I really enjoyed your last visit, Ava, I did. It's just that—"

"—I love how confident Josie is! Catherine can be very shy sometimes, you know. She's struggling to make friends, and it's breaking my heart."

Sylvie looked down. Ava knew she was being unfair, what with her taking the easy way out while Sylvie tried to tell her something unpleasant.

"Sorry, bit of an offload there. It's just been a bit of a tough week. Is she a happy girl? Josie, I mean. She looks like a very content soul."

"She is, yes. Sometimes I feel like I can't, you know, talk to her in a way she would listen to, if that makes sense?"

Yes, you and every other parent on the planet.

"I keep trying to talk to her, make her open up a bit," Sylvie said, " but then she will just clam up and look at me like I'm from another planet or something."

"What about your husband?"

"Michael is, yes, he's great," Sylvie said. Mentioning her husband had put a dampener on the conversation. "He is, Ava. He's so generous, and helpful, and practical, and…"

She sounded like she was describing her boss and not her partner. Ava chastised herself for bringing him up, but it was too late now. The damage was already done.

"Ava, I don't know if I can do this yet."

"It's okay, I know it's hard. I didn't think I could either, but I think I got spooked. As I mentioned in the letter."

Sylvie stared at her.

Of course, thought Ava. *She didn't get the letter.* She realised that Michael would have intercepted the words she wrote in confidence to Sylvie.

"I wrote to you, Sylvie, just after I almost had a car accident last year. And after we, Sean and I found…   never mind. It just made me think so much... too much, perhaps. It reminded me of that day at the lake. I think I must have nine lives or something. But what if something happened to me or what if Catherine did some exploring of her own? They're more inquisitive than we know. Even at this age."

"Ava, I had no idea. I'm so sorry. Michael is just a bit protective of us and likes to handle all the mail. I've been fragile recently and he probably just didn't want to upset me."

By now Ava just wanted to scream that no, it wasn't okay at all and that such things didn't happen in a marriage anymore. She relented, though, as she noticed Sylvie's shame, and focused on something else.

"Fragile? Is everything okay?"

"I guess. Well, I'm not sure, actually."

There they were, the confusion and the vacant stare again.

"Talk to me. You can trust me. We were friends for a long time."

"Well, I'm feeling a lot better now. The doctor said it's common to feel anxious as a mother and a wife. Not wanting to make mistakes, miss anything?"

"What are you worried about?"

"I don't know. Everything and nothing, really. It sounds crazy, I know, but Michael's always here, always happy to support me and remind me I just need to keep life simple. Focus on the things that matter. You know, my family and feeling safe at home," she explained. "Anyway, enough about me. How are you?"

"I... I think you were trying to tell me you don't want the girls to meet because Michael thinks it's a bad idea. Is that right?" Even saying these words out loud sparked Ava's rage again. She wondered why this man had such a massive say in her future.   Ava was troubled by the controlling claws he had sunk into Sylvie.

"Yes, yes, sorry. He thinks — we think our lives are settled, and Josie is happy with her world as it is."

"And you, Sylvie, what do you think?"

"There are moments, Ava," she started, cradling her mug in her hands. "Moments when I dream about the girls meeting and finding out about their connection. But don't you ever worry? If, you know, they'd hate us for it? For the deception? For separating them in the first place?"

"Of course I do. I worry more about them discovering it before we tell them ourselves. Also, I hate how we cannot be friends again until that day comes."

"Ava, we agreed to wait until we were both sure that it was the right time to tell the girls everything."

"Yes, but we also agreed that we would stay close enough to see each other often enough, and that didn't happen either, did it?

Sylvie shrank on herself with what looked like shame and Ava tried to tone her desperation down.

"Maybe we don't have to tell them everything, Sylvie. Maybe we just have to tell them something."

Ava could see the clouds lifting from Sylvie's eyes. Joy was written all over her face, a joy Ava remembered well. That and Sylvie's powerful spirit.

"Maybe we could tell the girls they're our daughters and nothing more?"

"What harm can it do?"

Although Sylvie remained quiet at this, Ava could read her face like a book, even after the years had passed. There was no doubting the signs of tempered excitement behind her eyes.

"I can't tell Michael. He would be upset if he thought we were meeting again."

Tread carefully, Ava thought. There was no point in scaring Sylvie off by offering her opinion on Michael.

"Okay, let's not tell him, then. Where shall we meet?"

Chapter 21

AVA

Stirlingshire, 2008

Ava arrived at the park about ten minutes early. There was just enough time to check the weather and decide how many layers of clothes Catherine would need. She wanted the day to be a calm one, but the clouds had other ideas and gathered in thick, dark grey masses as they approached the entrance to the adventure park. In any other circumstances, normal circumstances, two parents would simply pick up their phones and discuss re-arranging for another day. There was nothing normal about this occasion, though.

She remembered words that were exchanged between her and Sean the day before.

"We are just letting the girls meet up. Nothing more than that, just as the daughters of two good friends who haven't seen each other in a while. That's all."

"That's all for *now*?"

"Yes, I think it is."

"Ava, I know you," Sean said. "Once you set your sights on something, you will pursue it step by step. Are you telling me that if things don't go as planned with this cozy little play date, you're just going to call it a day? Put your plan on hold until the stars align again?"

"I don't know. I just, I just want to do what is right by everyone. We owe it to Catherine to know who might be there for her."

"Just like you owed Sylvie for pulling you out of the water all those years ago? The debt that defined the rest of your life as a friend and mother. The debt that made you hand over one of your babies."

His words came without warning, with enough power and ferocity to wreck actual damage.

She was shoving a raincoat into her rucksack when her phone lit up with an incoming text message.

-We're here. See you at the main entrance. Sx -

Ava looked at Catherine, who was blissfully unaware of the magnitude of that day. As far as she was concerned, it was all about sheer joy and playtime with another girl.

"What's her name, Mummy?" she asked.

"Sylvie's daughter is called Josie, darling."

"I hope she likes penguins. And giraffes. And ice cream!"

"I have a feeling she will."

The rain started as they approached the gate. Ava squeezed Catherine's hand and paused for a moment, undecided. Maybe they should go back to their car? She turned towards the parking lot, and a strange thought—a car in the distance seemed a bit too much in tune with her movements—occurred to her.

"Mum?"

Catherine was looking at her mum with impatience.

"Mum? Why have we stopped? *Mum!*"

"S—sorry, sorry, Catherine. I just thought I saw…"

"What? Mum! Can we just go?"

"Jacket, an extra jacket. Let's go back for—"

"*No.* I just want to go in now, please!"

Ava folded under the pressure. They went on, joining the crowd that passed under the entrance arch emblazoned with '*This Way for a Truly Wild Adventure*'. Still, the unsettling feeling of being watched kept niggling at her, despite her attempts to focus on what was about to happen.

And there they were. Standing together, just a mother with her daughter, waiting to meet their friends for a day out. How was it possible, Ava wondered, for something so important to look so normal?

You wanted this. You drove everyone down this path, now don't you dare lose your shit.

"Sweetie, this is my special friend, Sylvie, and this gorgeous young lady is Josie."

Catherine's gaze plummeted towards her feet, and she moved a little closer to Ava while Josie offered her a warm smile.

"Hi, I'm Josie! Do you like penguins?" Josie asked. She seemed the most capable of taking the lead, and maybe help Catherine overcome her shyness. "I like penguins. Did you know they are the fastest swimmers, even though they walk funny on land?"

Catherine chuckled, so Josie went on. "What's your favourite animal? I like things that swim and things that look cuddly."

"Penguins and giraffes are my favourite." Those words came in a faint tone, but she'd answered, regardless. It had taken Josie less than thirty seconds to elicit a response from Catherine.

"I like those too. I saw a girl on *Paint, Draw, Share* who was amazing at drawing them. Do you watch that?"

"Sometimes. When Mum and Dad are both working. It's fun."

It was now raining cats and dogs, and they followed the crowd toward the Sea Lion Theatre. It stunk of rotten fish and looked like a seaside resort, with kids dropping ice cream and bouncing around while their parents tried to restrain them.

Ava realised that she and Sylvie hadn't spoken to each other yet, and she could only hope that they were on the same page—or, at least, that Sylvie was not far behind.

Catherine still stuck to her side, using her as a safety blanket.

"Don't you think it's sad, Mummy, that the sea lions are not in the sea where they're supposed to be?"

Before Ava could answer, someone else intervened.

"They actually enjoy performing, and they were rescued from death because of injury or disease."

Josie's confidence was impressive, never mind her knowledge. Still, Sylvie shot Ava a look that seemed apologetic.

"Isn't that great to hear?" Ava said. "What a clever girl you are, Josie."

Smiling at her mother, Catherine settled back to enjoy the show, even if Ava could almost feel the envious admiration rising from her daughter like steam. As a child, Ava had known envy well. She remembered how it gripped her every time she left Sylvie's happy family to return home.

The show ended around noon, and they went to the main area of the park. The weather had cleared up, so they could start with their picnic. After laying their coats on a soggy bench, Ava fished out food from her shabby rucksack while Sylvie delved into her expensive-looking tote.

Picnic inadequacy. Didn't see that one coming, Ava thought. The different worlds they inhabited could be defined by the assortment of Waitrose's finest pasta salads and charcuterie sitting next to a family pack of sausage rolls.

Still, both girls ate quickly before Josie asked if they could play next to the picnic tables.

"Absolutely. You would love that, wouldn't you, Catherine?" It was more of a hope than a statement, but after some more gentle nudging, Catherine followed Josie towards the zip line queue, only turning back for a nod of approval.

The leftover rubbish went into a trash bag, and Ava darted towards the bins, walking fast to avoid spilling anything. Once again, she felt the weight of eyes on her and once again she redirected her attention elsewhere. *You're a mad cow, Ava.*

"She clearly loves her mum very much."

"Sorry?"

"Catherine. She adores you, Ava."

"As Josie adores you."

"Sometimes I'm not sure how much she needs me, you know? It's like she doesn't quite know how to? She's always looking for adventure rather than comfort."

Don't say it, please, don't say it.

"She's so like you, Ava." Too late. "So like her —"

"No, Sylvie. You are her mother, and she needs you as much as Catherine needs me."

"We just don't always, I don't know, connect? You know what I mean by that? I adore her and I know she loves me, I do. Just, sometimes it feels like there is a distance between us. Like we don't really *get* each other."

The emphasis Sylvie placed on 'get' hung in the air between them.

"They're young. Just remember that."

The women spoke to each other from the heart. As they watched the children discover their own friendship, Ava was reminded of a simpler time; before the weight of life bore down on them with a ferocity.

"How is it going with Sean?"

It had been too long since someone asked after him, and Ava didn't know what she was about to say.

"I'm... not sure. I think we're fine, but then it feels like he's somewhere else. You know, physically and emotionally. It makes me wonder whether he'd ever — never mind. I'm being paranoid."

"Whether he would what?"

"He loves me. I know he does. He just seems distracted, I guess. And, well, money is tight. He's not getting much work, and the little he has seems to involve late-evening meetings, which doesn't help."

Ava pulled herself from her own mind by pulling the zip of her jacket up to her neck and tucking her now cold hands in her pockets.

"Listen to me. I sound like some desperate housewife whose imagination is getting the better of her. As if Sean would have the energy to get himself —"

The words petered out into silence. Catherine was walking towards her with a panicked look on her face.

"Mum. Where's Josie?"

"Sweetheart, what do you mean? Josie was with you."

The fear and uncertainty that radiated from Catherine were enough of an answer. Sylvie paled, and she staggered to her feet. In the meantime, Catherine started talking.

"She said something about seeing someone and that she was going to the sweets machine, and would be back in a minute, but that was ten minutes ago, and she's not there, Mum. Mum, I'm sorry."

"Don't worry, Catherine. We will find her. She won't be far."

"Josie!" Ava watched as Sylvie circled the area in a frenzy, attracting the attention of other parents. "Josie! Josie!"

All she could do was join in and try to cover as much ground as possible, with a crying Catherine at her side. By now, other people were searching for Josie, too, united by a strange bond; in moments like these, it was irrelevant whose child was lost because people moved as one — irrelevant to everyone but Sylvie. It was *her* daughter and *her* terror.

"Mum."

"Not now, Catherine," Ava shot back. "You just need to help me look."

"But Mum, I've had an idea." Catherine had a strange expression on her face now. It felt calming, somehow. "I think I know where she might be. I think she might be in the woods over there."

She pointed to a small area dense with trees that divided the parking lot from the picnic section.

"Why would she be there, Catherine?"

Her face was still. She seemed confident in what her instinct was telling her, and it was hard to ignore it. "I love to play in the woods, Mum. I feel safe beside the big trees. I know it sounds silly, but maybe Josie likes them, too?"

It was worth a try.

Ava turned to Sylvie, whose features were distorted by fear. "Sylvie, you stay at the table just in case she comes back. Catherine's had an idea."

"She what? Don't tell me to sit still. This is my child missing. *Mine*!" she spat.

"Trust me, please. We will find her."

In the background, a loudspeaker was making an announcement. Parents listened on and held their own children a little closer.

"Come with me," Ava said to Catherine, grabbing her daughter's hand and sprinting towards the trees. She had no reason to trust a hunch of a seven-year-old, and yet she did. Catherine did have the advantage of being Josie's twin, after all.

It was late spring, and the woodland was littered with a sea of yellow and purple, daffodils and crocuses that seemed to lighten up the path.

Where now?

Ava knew there was a small lake nearby. It was fenced off from the park, but the thought cast its barbs in her brain, and refused to leave. *Not the water. Not the water.* But Catherine was holding her hand, leading her with a firm grip — maybe for the first time in her life.

Then the tension in Catherine's hand gave way.

"I can see her pretty dress over there. Can you see it?"

"Where? Are you sure? Is that a flower bed?"

"No, Mum. That is the dress Josie is wearing. I know because I love it, too."

She was right. Josie was sitting among the flowers, unaware of all the chaos that was erupting around her. A small, innocent, and content child picking daffodils.

Ava rushed towards her, almost tripping up in the undergrowth.

"Oh, thank God, Josie. Are you okay?"

"I'm picking flowers for Catherine. She said she liked the ones on my dress, so I wanted to surprise her."

"Sweetheart, come here. Your Mum is worried sick," Ava said, taking Josie's hand and ringing Sylvie at the same time.

"Is Mum cross? I thought I saw someone, that's all. When I couldn't see them anymore, I thought I would play in the woods."

Josie looked anxious, but Sylvie was already answering the phone. "Ava?"

"She's safe. She's here. In the forest. Picking flowers."

The line went dead right away, and less than a minute later, Sylvie was tearing across the field, half smiling and half crying. By the time Sylvie had reached them, Ava and Catherine had formed a protective embrace around Josie. Tears streaming from Catherine's face, she was turning her head away in what looked like shame.

"Darling, it's okay. Everyone is safe and well."

"But it was my fault, Mummy. I was supposed to look after her."

"No, no Catherine. You were… you were supposed to look after each other."

They sat together, motionless, and a wave of relief washed over her face, transforming every part of her expression in a moment.

Later that afternoon, as they were about to part ways, Ava took a moment to watch the girls saying their goodbyes. Friends for about five hours, they had bonded already; they would need each other in a way only twins can understand. Even those who didn't even know they were twins.

"We must go, Ava. I've got enough explaining to do as it is. Heaven knows what I will go home to. I can't be late," Sylvie said. Her hands were shaking as she reached her car.

"I'm so sorry to have upset you, Mummy," Josie said. "I didn't mean to. It's just weird because I thought I saw… oh, never mind."

"Who did you think you saw, Josie?"

"I thought I saw Daddy."

Sylvie's face turned white. She bundled her daughter into the car, slammed the doors, and reversed backward, barely pausing to wave as they went.

Chapter 22

AVA

Edinburgh, 2008

It was just after five o'clock when Ava and Catherine arrived home, exhausted and Ava craved some adult company. Feeling for her phone in her handbag, she sent a message to Sean.

Shall we get some time together, just the two of us tonight, Sean? The girls. They met today. It was almost perfect.

The response was not quick to appear and was lukewarm in tone.

That's a relief. Not sure when I'll be back.

That's a relief.   Christ, Sean, it's a bit more than a relief. How does he not get how massive this is? As the clock ticked towards eight and Catherine dragged herself to bed, Ava could picture how her evening would go. Just her and her thoughts, her fears, and her plans to wrangle with.

Before she knew it, sleep was luring her into its cozy embrace, and she let herself drift off.

It could have been minutes or hours later when she came to; Sean was there, taking the remote and the half-eaten tub of *Pringles* away from her.

Waking up had always been hard on her, and the fact that Sean knew about it just heightened her rage. "Getting pretty used to spending them on my own. I had a husband who liked to hang out, you see."

"I'm making something to eat. Tempting as it is to stay for this chat, I think I'll let you fight with your own shadow for a while. Shall I make you some pasta?"

"Don't be an arse, Sean."

"It's just pasta. It might not be that bad."

"You know what I mean. I thought we were okay. I thought I could rely on you, that you'd see me — us — through this. Why are you not asking me how it went today? Can't you see what a huge step this was for m—   "

"Enough, Ava! Enough!"

Hearing Sean raise his voice for the first time in ages startled her. She took a breath and watched him as he put down the knife on the chopping board and took a firm hold of the kitchen worktop as if to steady himself for impact. His next words were delivered with clarity that made Ava take notice.

"You need to calm down or I refuse to talk to you."

Relenting at her husband's words, Ava pulled out a chair and sat at the kitchen table, and let him continue uninterrupted.

"Do you really want to know where I've been going all these evenings?"

"I don't know, do I?" she asked, petrified by both his question and the look of embarrassment on his face.

"I've been seeing a bloody shrink, Ava. Or, to give you the official terminology, I've been seeking psychological help for what I've been reliably informed is a *pretty nasty case of post-traumatic stress disorder.*"

"Fuck. I… I wasn't expecting… You've, you've what?"

"Didn't see that one coming now, did you?"

"I don't understand, Sean."

"That's because you're too busy chasing after your friend to know what's happening on your own doorstep. I can't believe you thought I absorbed a life-changing secret as if it was nothing."

"No, of course not, but you've been so distant —"

"Christ, Ava, you've had seven years to deal with it. That and deciding on when I got to find out."

It was true. She had inflicted deep trauma on her husband. He was exhibiting all the signs.

"Sean, why couldn't you just…"

"What? Talk about it? Really?"

"Yes?"

"Because you have been so single-mindedly focused on Sylvie and our daughter's twin that you have had little time to spare for anyone else."

A crushing feeling blossomed in her chest upon hearing that. Sean had always been there. Mr Resilient. Teflon man. Why did he have to be so human and fragile now?

"I'm so—Sean, I'm so sorry. I thought because you came back to me, to us, I guess I thought you had come to terms with everything."

"No. I just couldn't come to terms with being alone while I tried to make sense of all this." Sean paused and took a long breath before continuing.

"Mostly, I just wanted to make you happy."

There was a vulnerability in Sean's words that humbled Ava. She watched him let everything rise to the surface.

"It's like... I don't know, it's like you girls have to fight each other's battles together."

Of course, he needed to work this out. It was at that moment that a light bulb seemed to switch on in Ava's head. It shone a light on the depth of need for each other that two friends can have. A bond cemented not by marriage, but by a shared coming of age. A time of growing and understanding the world around you. A time of needing another human being by your side to make life a little less overwhelming.

"She saved my life. She could have drowned herself, but she saved me and ruined her chances of becoming a mother."

"Yes, I know. It looks like it's been casting a shadow over you since it happened."

Sean's words stung Ava. Why can he not understand why I had no other choice? It compelled her to ask painful questions, but she shuddered at the prospect of the answer.

"Do you not want a future with me anymore? Do you regret coming back to us?"

"No, I don't regret it, I think. I just need the space to come to terms with everything without you picking fights."

"I get it, Sean. It's just, it hurts to know that she's struggling to make friends and I wonder if it's possible to miss someone you've never known?"

He looked at Ava, silent and deeply unsettling.

"What, no smart dismissal, then?" she asked, pushing further. Still no words came from Sean. Just the faintest glistening of tears appeared in his eyes.

"I've been so lost in my head, worrying about Catherine and Sylvie. Guess I kind of put you last; let you drift away from me."

"I've not gone anywhere, though. I just needed someone to talk to as well."

Ava smiled at him and watched as he busied himself with the pasta and the pots. "And has it, you know, helped?"

"I don't know yet. Hey, at least I'm able to tell my shrink I'm struggling, too."

Ava's thoughts drifted back to the day's events. She had to tell Sean what had happened, even if she was more concerned about Sylvie. What did she go home to?

Should I call her? Or would that just make things worse?

"There was something else. About today."

"Oh man, what now? Did a penguin look at you funny, or did you drop your handbag in the hippo's tank?"

"We thought we had lost Josie at one point. She disappeared. Vanished just like that."

"Jesus, Ava, that's a big deal."

"But it was ok. We found her. She was just picking flowers in the forest. For Catherine, apparently."

Sean was sighing; Ava guessed he was struggling to keep up.

"That's a bit odd, though, isn't it, Ava? Why would she just disappear like that without telling Sylvie? Especially if you were all having this nice, perfect time together?"

"No, no, I mean it, Sean, it was weird. And the oddest bit was when... when we were leaving, I heard Josie say that she ran away because she thought she saw her dad."

Sean raised an eyebrow but didn't look up from stirring the pasta. "So what, Edinburgh's busiest lawyer followed his family to watch them eating their lunch? For real?"

"I know — it sounds ridiculous. I also had an odd feeling, though, and some men need to control everything."

"Ava, stop. If I had a pound for every time Catherine convinced us she saw someone she knew in the weirdest of places... They're all the same at that age. Wild imaginations! Now. are you going to eat with me tonight or do I need to call my non-existent girlfriend?"

Ava followed him to bed that night, desperate to be close to him and feel the warmth of his touch and the reassurance of his body. Something made her stop at Catherine's bedroom door. Her book had slipped from her grasp, so Ava tiptoed inside to put it away; on her bedside table, Ava noticed that a handful of misshapen daffodils had been rammed into a plastic cup.

I was picking them for you, Catherine.

Josie's words rang in Ava's mind, and she felt more compelled than ever to bring the girls together. Acting on instinct, Ava curled up next to Catherine until the rhythmic sounds of her breathing lulled her to sleep.

Chapter 23

SYLVIE & AVA

Glasgow 2008

Sylvie was confident that Michael knew nothing about the true nature of their trip. In his eyes, it would have been a normal day at the zoo, and he wouldn't question something so innocent.

"Let's not tell Daddy about today, huh? We don't want him to be upset, do we?" Although she hated to lie to her, she hoped that one day her daughter would understand.

"Okay, Mummy," Josie said. She could probably feel the desperation in Sylvie's voice. "Mummy, did you hear me when I said I thought I saw Daddy at the park?"

Her heart sank with the belief that Michael's presence was so overwhelming it had taken control of Josie's imagination, too. "Sweetheart, Daddy would not have been there. You know he was at work."

"But, Mum, I—"

"Enough, Josie. Go and do your homework now."

Michael would return in less than an hour, and lately she had to work hard to get back into his good books. Something was rattling him, and the safest option was to be invisible and subservient. The thrill of keeping something from him helped her self-confidence, though.

At six-thirty pm, Michael walked through the door. He was a bit earlier than expected, and Sylvie had not finished cooking his dinner. That wasn't good.

"How was your day, sweetheart?" she asked, trying to deflect his attention as she turned up the oven and threw some rice in a pan when he wasn't looking.

"Testing. I'm hungry, Sylvie. Is there something that's been slowing you down today?"

"Slowing me? I was expecting you at—" One look from him was enough to silence her. "I'm sorry. I promise it won't be long. I'm sure Josie would love to tell you about her day while I cook."

"I'm sure she would. Come and tell Daddy how your trip without me went, Josie."

"Michael, it was just the zoo and you work so hard we can't always do these things together. No harm came of it."

"No harm you say?" Nausea rose within her as the expression on his face turned sinister. "Well, my dear, I guess that depends on what you would call harmful."

"...Michael?"

Oh God, he knows. He must have got it out of Josie when I wasn't around. Or is he just messing with my mind again?

"Because, you see, quite a lot of parents would consider it harmful to lose their child for half an hour, don't you think?" Her heart felt like it was going to explode. She took a deep breath, trying to find some inner strength before letting the words escape.

"Were you there? Michael? Did you follow us?"

Sylvie couldn't quite believe she was asking him if *he* had followed them to spy on them. Then, had he — he'd somehow lured Josie away before vanishing, sending Sylvie into a panic.

"You didn't, Michael. Surely you couldn't have been there?"

Michael came so close they were standing next to each other, eye to eye. She could smell his acrid breath and see beads of sweat appearing on his forehead. His eyes were bloodshot. *Rage*, she thought.

"Sylvie, I am everywhere. I need you to know that."

Silence followed his words. The kind of silence that seems louder than anything else.

"Mum? Dad? Is everything okay?"

Josie was standing at the kitchen door. Sylvie didn't know how long she'd been there, and she could tell that Michael didn't care. He'd had his say. He didn't speak during dinner either while Sylvie busied herself with menial tasks, wanting to avoid making eye contact. Her hands were still shaking when she dried the dishes with a towel.

#

The letter appeared on Ava's doormat a month later.

Dear Ava,

I know you have your reasons for reconnecting with me and attempting to introduce Catherine to Josie. Unlike you, I didn't want to do this so soon, but I went along with it because you are my friend. It has to end here, now. After much thought and discussion with Michael, we have decided that it is too disruptive, upsetting, and unnecessary to pursue this reunion, and we need you to keep your distance for now. Life has dealt you a tough hand and money might be tight, but I worry that having seen the means we have at our disposal, your motives for pursuing a reunion may be a financial reason. Please do not contact me or Josie again. We will do so when we are ready, but I don't expect it to be anytime soon.
Wishing you the best for the future.
Your friend, Sylvie

Ava crumpled it and threw it in the nearest bin. She used to ache with jealousy at the blissful life Sylvie had when they were younger. Now, in adulthood, Ava was beginning to understand how far the tables had turned. Her friend needed protection more than ever. She couldn't let her down.   Ava stared at her laptop screen for a few moments, pretending to work while Sean watched some football match — watched and shouted obscenities at it every so often.

"Sean, I'm going back tomorrow after dropping Catherine off. I must. And I'm going on my own."

His gaze did not leave the TV, and she did not know if he heard her. The truth was, it made no difference anyway.

#

This time, Michael was waiting for her. She sensed he'd been expecting her, in a way, because his car was in the driveway, parked outside rather than in their pretentious garage. To her, it was a detail that screamed of arrogance and self-confidence. Even from a young age, he was a man who knew how to shore up his defenses in the face of an enemy approach

Ava hesitated to gather her thoughts and wondered if she should feel nervous. He would like that, she was sure. She also wondered about how simpler life would be if she just left it alone; sooner or later, Catherine would make some friends while she and Sean could go back to their happy marriage. Sure, it would hurt for a while, but in the end, she would learn to accept it.

Still, she wanted more. More for herself, and perhaps more for her daughter, too.

When Ava got out of the car, she noticed the edge of a shadow moving across the room. *It's a bloody cat,* she thought. *A judgmental and suspicious cat, that's for sure, but just a cat.*

Still, as if on cue, Michael opened the door moments after Ava rang the bell.

"Hi, Ava."

She was met by a physical presence that should probably have been intimidating. He had always been tall, but he had bulked out over the years with muscle tone. Everything about him spoke of dominance. There was no doubting it: the Alpha male was present.

He offered her his hand, and the strength behind it somehow belittled her. She had to remind herself that this visit was on her terms, so she shouldn't be expecting any niceties.

"It's good to see you again. You look well."

Still a tosser then, just a bit richer.

"Hi, Michael. It seems like you've… done well for yourself," she answered, aware she wasn't that able to fake politeness. It was something Sean loved about her.

"Is Sylvie in?" Ava said after no invitation to step inside came forth.

"No, I'm afraid she's not."

"Oh, okay. Do you know when she might be back?"

"Nope. It could be a while."

Well, this is going well.

Blood rushed to her neck, but she pressed on. "What about Josie?"

"They're together, and I'm afraid I've got to take a work call. I'm so sorry you've come all this way for nothing. Perhaps if you had called before, we might have been—"

"Ah, but the problem is that Sylvie doesn't seem to get my messages."

"Does she not? How odd. Now if you'll just excuse me…"

"Daddy, who's that?"

There she was, the girl who was supposed to be away.

"Get back to your homework. Josie," he said, but it was too late. Even the mere sight of her felt heart-stopping.

"Hello, Josie, how are you, darling? It's lovely to see you again."

"Ava! Daddy, it's Ava, the lady we met at the Safari Park! Is Catherine here too? Are you here for a visit?"

"Well, sweetheart, I was here to see Mummy, but your daddy tells me she's not in."

"She's only gone to the shops. Can you wait with me until she gets back? I can show you my room. Did you bring Catherine? I told Catherine about the twinkly lights all around my bed and stars in the ceiling, and I think she liked that!"

Mesmerized by Josie's babbling, Ava watched as she tucked her hair behind her ears—just like Catherine did.

"Josie, go back to your room. I think Ava is in a hurry, which is a shame—"

"Not in a hurry, no!" Anger at his easy dismissal of Josie paired with self-confidence grew inside her. "That's a very sweet offer. I'd love to see your room if your daddy is happy with that?"

Michael had to let her in. It was plain he was brimming with rage—his glare spoke volumes—but he managed to keep up his pretence and act like a charming host.

Soon, Josie took Ava's hand and led her upstairs. At first, Ava didn't think much of Josie's room: bathed in multiple shades of pink, it featured glittering stationery and bookshelves kitted out with books. It wasn't just any room, though.

The colours, the style, the way her clothes were hanging in the glass-fronted wardrobe, or how she had arranged her cuddly toys and shoes? It was a mirror image of Catherine's own room, just larger and more expensive.

Of course.

Ava remembered sitting on her front porch, five months pregnant and uncomfortable while she read the tale of the Minnesota twins. Separated at birth and reunited at thirty-nine, they had both married twice to wives with the same names, they both named their children James, drove the same car, and took holidays on a Florida beach. That had made her decision a little easier to bear.

The sound of a door opening brought Ava back to reality. Leaving Josie in her room to search for a book, she peered over the staircase banister just in time to see Sylvie. Michael, leaning against the door to the hallway, was looking at her, too. There was something menacing about his presence that made Ava want to scream at Sylvie; fear held her body rigid, though, and she watched as he brought his head closer to hers.

"Nice of you to join us," he said, his voice icy cold.

"Michael! You gave me such a fright!"

"A fright? But this is your home, Sylvie. I realise that you've been out for so long you may have forgotten that, though."

"I went to the shops, like I do every Saturday at two o'clock in the afternoon, remember?"

"You do, but it doesn't take you two hours. Did you meet anyone interesting?"

"I just went for a walk along the river. It was a lovely afternoon, and I needed the fresh air."

Michael kept his eyes on his wife, who remained rooted to the spot with her head and eyes falling towards the floor.

"And is there something wrong with the fresh air of our garden?"

Ava felt sick. This was her dearest friend he was talking to. She meant to walk back to Josie's bedroom, but before she could move, Josie came running.

"Ava, Ava, come back! I thought you were going to read me a book!"

Both Michael and Sylvie's gazes landed on her. Michael seemed to stand his ground, grinning like a bully, while Sylvie seemed full of embarrassment and fear. She looked like she'd rather be anywhere but there.

Ava took a few tentative steps down the winding staircase, thinking as fast as possible.

"Sylvie. Hi. I'm sorry to just turn up like this, but I was explaining to Michael that I've been trying—"

"Ava was getting to know our daughter while she waited for you. Why don't you girls hang out? I'll make some drinks." *Your mind games don't fool me.*

"Mummy, come up here with us! Ava's going to read some of my schoolbooks with me."

Sylvie appeared to jump at the chance to escape and made her way upstairs. When her daughter was distracted by rifling through her bookshelves, she turned to Ava.

"Ava, it's so lovely to—"

"I'm sorry. Sean told me not to."

"Yes. I'm not sure it's a good idea."

"I know, I got your letter, and it just broke my heart."

"My what?"

"I need to respect your judgement and opinions, I know, but… I just had to… I just wanted to give you another chance," she said, watching Sylvie dissolve into a ball of shame. "It's okay. I'm not angry. I can understand why you don't want Catherine and Josie to spend time together, that you think it's too soon. I don't agree with it, but I'm willing to accept it."

"Ava, stop."

"As for the other stuff about me, and, and my motives? Really? Do you even remember who I am?"

Silence met Ava's tirade. Not a word came from the friend who had once been her soulmate.

"…Sylvie?" she started, and then it hit her. *Surely not? It's too much?*

"That bastard downstairs wrote that letter, didn't he?"

"Ava, please don't speak like that in front of Josie. He's just trying to protect—"

"Protect you, Sylvie? Is that what you really think? The man is trying to control your life!"

"Mummy? Is everything okay?" Josie asked. She'd stopped perusing the shelves and was now looking at them for answers.

"Of course, sweetie. Ava was just telling me a crazy story about someone we both used to know. Why don't you pop downstairs and see if Daddy wants some help—there's a sweetheart."

Once they were alone, Ava knew she had to try and find what was left of her friend. It was her turn to rescue Sylvie and pull her back to the surface.

"Sylvie, I knew you wouldn't write those words to me. I only wanted to bring the girls together, but I also need to know that you're all right."

"Look at me, Ava. Of course, I'm all right! I live in a beautiful house with my perfect daughter and a husband who would do anything to protect us. Why would I not be happy? Why can't you leave us be?"

"I know you. Even after all these years, I know you better than anyone. And this… he… he's not good for you."

"Is this because he ended up with me instead of you? Are you jealous?"

"Christ. Sylvie. That was low."

"God. I'm sorry. I didn't mean that, but I think you should leave," Sylvie said. She was walking away, and Ava knew she had pushed too far. Sean was right by saying Ava kept going at it until something broke. Well, now it did.

"Sylvie, I'm sorry too. I know—"

"You know nothing about my life. Nothing. And I want you to leave."

Ava followed her out, desperate to cling to her. It was her last chance.

"Don't do this. I can help you. Both of you."

"Everything okay, ladies?"

There he was. Looming once again in the shadows.

"Ava just remembered she had to get home, actually."

"What a shame."

Michael smiled at Ava. It made her boil up inside with rage, even if she was getting kicked out. All she could do now was pray that Sylvie and Josie were safe. They were not her responsibility, but her instinct said otherwise.

As she pulled up outside her small but uncomplicated house, back to her flawed but loving husband, she saw a note poking out of her jacket's pocket. It was handwritten on expensive paper.

Dear Ava,

I tried to give you a subtle warning of the chaos I can and will cause, should you attempt to disrupt my family. You're not capable of looking after them for one day, as you've recently proven. I saw everything that day when you let my daughter wander into the woods, to be lost or taken by a stranger. Luckily, I was watching over her. I need you to know that nothing can be hidden from me. I urge you to leave your family alone, or this path you are choosing to tread will not lead to the happy destination you have planned.

Michael Miller.

Chapter 24

AVA

Glasgow 2008

Ava sat rooted to the driver's seat, a mixture of nausea and fury rising inside her.
She knew she was dealing with a disturbing man, but she didn't yet know how low he would go.

Christ, Ava, what is wrong with you? You need to walk away now.
Her thoughts were dancing in every conceivable direction as
she composed herself before getting out of her car. Could she
pull off some sort of dramatic intervention by kidnapping
Sylvie and Josie by dawn? She had whipped herself into a
manic frenzy. Knowing that she would risk losing Sean's
support if she did not calm down and think rationally, Ava
closed her eyes and took low, slow breaths, willing her heart
rate to return to normal. She knew that losing her shit would
help no one, and she couldn't afford to push Sean away again.
(But, whether it was her fury or mother's instinct driving her
forward, it was there - by her side - going nowhere).
Sean greeted her in the hallway as soon as she walked
through the door.
"Ava? I was starting to worry. How did it go?"
"Don't ask."
"I just did. What happened?"
"What happened is that that man is a twisted, controlling arse,
far more than I could have imagined."
"Ava, please calm—"
"Don't tell me to calm down, Sean. You should have seen me
two hours ago. Read this."
Ava thrust Michael's letter at Sean and waited. Colour began
to drain from his face as he skimmed it; once he reached the
end, he let out a long, deep breath.
"Holy shit, this man is a grade-A psycho."
Ava just looked at him and folded her arms in a self-satisfied
manner, albeit a reluctant one.
"Do I have to say I told you so?" Sean said. Then, visibly
annoyed by her refusal to admit her mistake, he went on;
"Ava, this is serious. You need to back off."

"Back off? Are you kidding me? They need me, they need *us* more than ever. What kind of life is that? They're trapped in a gilded cage with someone who wants to control them. Sylvie couldn't even take a walk without him suggesting she was about to run away. Which, by the way, she would have every right to do."

"So, what do you suggest we do, Ava? We can't call the police, he has committed no crime."

"Does this letter not count as threatening? He admitted to setting up Josie's disappearance. We all assumed Josie was imagining it when she said she saw Daddy, but she was right."

Ava waited for a reaction, remembering Sean's earlier dismissal of the incident as the ramblings of an imaginative child. He shifted in his seat and began to shake his foot around in circles, a nervous trait she didn't miss.

"Shit, he was there the whole time, hiding in the bushes like some stalker."

"Exactly. Who does that to their own child? He must have attracted her attention and then hid to watch Sylvie's panic."

"You need to stay away from this man."

"He's batshit crazy, there's no doubt about that, but I still don't know what we can do. She is his wife, a grown adult, and she has to make her own decisions."

"And Josie? What about her?"

"You told me Sylvie and Michael are her legal guardians. All official, remember? And you can be sure he'll have his name on ALL the paperwork. If we get mixed up in that, we could end up in a whole world of trouble."

"But Josie is my —" Ava cut herself off. She couldn't say it; it would be unfair to everyone involved.

"So is Catherine. And I don't know if I'm willing to take that risk. I'm sorry."

"That's the whole point, Sean. I can't stop thinking about Catherine. How would I feel if it was Catherine living in that house? I chose to let Josie go because she seemed somehow stronger. Should she be punished for being a content newborn?"

"I know. I know, but you can't go back now. Sometimes mistakes have to be left alone. Do you understand what I'm saying?"

"But we'd help Sylvie and Josie escape, and surely that's the right thing to do?"

"Ava, you are not listening to me. You have to let go."

"I can't. That's the problem," she said. Tears were streaming down her face and she was scared to make eye contact with him. Looking at him right now would force her to back down. "I know what that feels like to live like that, and I can't let Michael get away with it."

Desperation was thick in her voice. After a while, he sank back in his chair and sighed.

"Well, I'm asking you again, then. What is your plan?"

Ava swallowed hard and poured him a drink.

#

Ava's plan was simple. She would inform Sylvie of Michael's threats, highlight his manipulative-narcissist side, and convince her to leave. Sean pointed out that, while the plan was indeed simple, she'd failed to consider all the potential obstacles.

"I think you might underestimate everyone involved here," he said.

Top of the list of Sean's concerns was the fact that Sylvie would not return any calls or texts. They would never reach her, giving him a reason to tighten the locks even further. Turning up on their doorstep again was out of the question, as it would probably lead to either an arrest or a restraining order.

"I need to keep busy. I need time to think this through."

After she began to pick up dirty socks and towels, Ava got distracted by the urge to enter her daughter's bedroom instead. Cushions, clothes, and soft toys were in their place, just like she had seen in Josie's bedroom. Her drawings were everywhere, instead. Under her bed, stuffed down the side of her armchair, stacked in small piles under books — and they offered the solution she was searching for. The way she could reconnect the girls in a safe way.

She caught her husband's eye again, aware of the self-satisfied look on her own face.

"Sean, I know how to get through to her."

"To whom?"

"I'm going to use that drawing program Catherine's obsessed with — you know, *Paint, Draw, Share* — to communicate with Josie ."

"You're what?" Sean said, wearing his familiar *I have no idea what you're talking about* expression.

"That kids' TV program. A bunch of kids send in their artwork and, if it's chosen, they appear on it and talk about what they've drawn."

"I'm still in the dark, Ava."

"I heard Catherine and Josie talk about it at the Safari Park. Josie watches it, too, and she does so with her mum. Like clockwork, she says."

"So, your plan is to convince them through the TV."

"Can you dial down the sarcasm?   This could work."

"You've lost it."

"No. This is my only option. It must work. I've been so focused on their separation that I've forgotten what they have in common. They're twins, for Christ's sake. I have to use that."

"All right, I'm listening. Go on."

"They're still young and they share simple, pleasurable stuff, and the stuff that makes them happy is all about them, so Michael would never notice."

"I don't think I'm keeping up with you yet, but that aside, what about Catherine? Will you tell her about her role in this master plan?"

"Catherine just needs to send in something, then talk about it. Then, fingers crossed, Josie and Sylvie will see it." Sean's nervous foot tapping had started again, but she pressed on, fuelled by her perceived genius. "You've seen her drawing. I doubt she'll need much encouragement to send in one of them. And then, well, we can take it from there."

"So, you will not ask her to draw a mother and child fleeing from a monster into the open arms of a guardian angel who looks like you?"

"I have a feeling that Catherine's art will be enough."

"Your mind works in strange ways."

"Well, something in my head convinced me to spend my life with you; you could be onto something."

Ava knew that her husband could read her like a book; she was too far down the path and too determined to be dissuaded. Whether he was just coming along for the ride and trying to keep everything on track, she adored him for his aversion to conflict.

Chapter 25

SYLVIE

Glasgow, two months later

Sylvie could feel Josie's eyes locked on her mother's face as they drove home from school. She played with the car radio a little, making a fuss about picking a fun song to sing along to. Anything at all to distract from the turmoil in her own head that she feared was threatening to give her away.

"What shall we do when we get home today, my darling?"

"Come on, Mum! What day is this?"

"Oh, sweetheart, I'm sorry. What have I forgotten? It's not the dancing club, is it? No, it's Wednesday. What do you mean?"

"Mum, it's Wednesday. You let me watch the TV after school on a Wednesday, remember?"

"You got me, sweetie. Mum needs more sleep, it seems. Of course. I'll grab the snacks, you get comfy on the sofa, and I'll be right in to join you."

Later on, while Sylvie was pulling some popcorn kernels from the larder, she heard a piercing squeal. Kernels flew everywhere as she dropped the bag, her heart almost leaping out of her chest.

"Josie? Josie, what's wrong? Where are you—"

"Mum! *Mum*, come quick, now! It's Catherine!"

Catherine? What? Where? Oh, God, is she on our doorstep?

"Mum! *Now*!"

"Good grief, child, what's with the wailing? What on earth do you mean, *it's Catherine*? Where is Cath—"

Sylvie stopped as she saw Catherine on the TV screen, holding up a series of drawings and talking to the show host. Just in the corner of the shot there was Ava, sitting next to her and beaming with pride.

"—everyone, this is Catherine Peterson from Edinburgh. Catherine is a very special guest on today's show because she has not one, but three beautiful pictures to share with all the young artists out there. Why don't you tell us about them, Catherine?"

Catherine shuffled in her chair, looked at her mum, and then seemed to rally herself for the job at hand.

"So, this first picture is of me at home, with my mum, my dad and our cat, Murphy. I drew this one a while ago after we read *The Tiger Who Came To Tea* because Murphy is a ginger cat that likes to eat a lot and sometimes reminds me of a tiger."

The host giggled on cue, and Sylvie could see it helped Catherine relax.

And, who is sitting next to you in this picture? Is it a friend from school?

"I... I don't know, really. Just someone I drew in the picture. I guess I thought it's nicer to have someone to sit next to."

A few spontaneous *awws* trickled around the studio. Some parents had a look of sympathy on their faces as they heard of that imaginary addition to the family.

"Wonderful," the host said. "And what about your next painting, Catherine?"

"It's a chalk drawing."

"My apologies, sweetheart. Of course, it is. And who is in this one?"

"Just me."

"What are you up to here? It looks like you might be in school, is that right?"

"Yes, I'm in my school playground. That's where I drew this; I was watching the other children play, and they looked so happy. I just wanted to draw them."

"What games do you play with your friends at break time? The colours are beautiful!"

"I don't."

As soon as the words left the presenter's mouth, Sylvie couldn't help but feel resentment at a host who had already forgotten Catherine's name, it seemed.

"I don't play with them, really. I draw. A lot. I like to imagine what it would be like to have a friend to play with all the time," Catherine said, squeezing her mother's hand tighter and tighter.

Through the studio lighting, Sylvie saw Ava had the same self-loathing expression she had seen so often. *What the hell, Ava?*

" —Josie?"

"Yes? It's a bit sad, isn't it, Mum? Is it making you sad?"

"Josie, did you tell Catherine and Ava that you watch this program?"

"Yes, I told them we watch it together and that it makes us happy, but this is making me sad today."

"I think we should turn it off for now," Sylvie said.

"Why does Catherine not play with her friends at school?"

"Oh, honey, I'm sure she does. She maybe just wants to sit a game out now and then. Lovely girls like Catherine have lots of friends."

The squeaking voice of the TV host cut through their exchange. "Well then, we think it's beautiful, don't we, art lovers? Shall we move on to your last picture?"

The host stared into the distance, looking a little nervous. Somewhere, a researcher was hiding in shame at the lack of both background research and prep. Did no one tell them that children couldn't fake it? They told life as it was, without the glitter and pom poms. Still, the program went on.

"Tell us about this one, can you? The team was impressed with it — it looks like you're having lots of fun here!"

"I was."

Catherine remained economical with her words, and the atmosphere was now loaded with tension.

"And why was that, my dear?"

"It was the best day I've had… probably ever! It was the day I made a special new friend at the park. We played all day and had so much fun, except for when we lost her in the woods. That was okay in the end because she thought she saw her dad, but her mum said it wasn't her dad and we had found her by then, so it didn't matter, anyway."

Sylvie could see that Catherine's long string of words had left the host stunned like a fox in headlights. Regardless, she raised a groomed eyebrow and let Catherine continue.

"And these bright colours here, do you see them?"

"Hm."

Catherine was not convinced by her nodding.

"No, here — look where my finger is." By now, she was holding her painting up and jabbing at the bottom section, which was awash with spots of lilac and pink. It looked like a junior version of Monet's water lilies.

"I do. Tell us about those."

"Those were the flowers that Josie picked for me. I kept them in a vase next to my bed until Mummy said they were smelling funny."

Another flood of sighs and *awws* went around the audience. This was a rollercoaster of emotions for a five-minute teatime segment. Josie and Sylvie were both glued to the screen, though.

"Mum, Mum, she's talking about us. About me. The flowers, the day at the park, it's *so* cool!"

"It is."

"Did you know she was going to be there? Did you want to keep it a secret, a surprise for me, Mum?"

Sylvie wanted to be angry at Ava for using Catherine to send her a message, but there was no doubt it was working. She drifted into a trance, connecting with Catherine's words as if she was sitting right in front of her.

We hear you, sweetheart. We do.

Sylvie heard the words in her own head, but wanted to tell Catherine in person.

"Well, I don't know about anyone else here, but I think you are a very talented young artist, er, Catherine," the host said. "Audience, do we agree?"

Part of the audience responded encouragingly enough, while the rest looked relieved to leave the girl's melancholy behind. In the comfort of her own home, Sylvie was silent, unmoving, and lost in her own mind.

"Mum, please, can we see Catherine again? Please. She said she's lonely... and sad. That makes me sad!" Josie started tugging on Sylvie's arm, snapping her out of her reverie. "Mum... can you hear me? It makes me really sad to think that she has no special friends at school."

Sylvie knew she had to see to her chores before Michael came back, but she felt like she was wading through treacle. It wasn't just Catherine who had been speaking to them — she could hear Ava behind every word, and, not for the first time, she insisted on being heard.

Okay, Ava, you win. You always were the stubborn, smart one.

Deep down, Sylvie wondered whether Ava's stunt meant to ignite the guilt she'd been wrestling with since she got entrusted with Josie.

"Take her in your arms, hold her tight," Ava had said that day, overcome with emotions. She had given birth to two perfect babies who would be loved and cherished forever — just not together as nature intended.

She remembered spending countless hours discussing their plan. It was a simple one, as Ava had done her research. She knew the rules for private adoption in Scotland inside and out.   It would have to begin with a fostering arrangement, which could lead in time to private adoption. These were just words, though. Paperwork. Procedures and legalities. None of that mattered as much as the result. Two children raised by best friends who had enough love to go around between them. Every instinct in her body told her that what her child lacked in a genetic connection to her parents, they would make up for in love and affection.

"How can I ever repay you, Ava?"

"I owe you my life. There is nothing to repay. Just promise me you will never look back; only forward, for the sake of your daughter. We're mothers now. Both of us," Ava had said once. "I want them to know each other when they're growing up. Friends, if not sisters."

"I agree. As long as they're not too similar, I think we can get away with it, no questions asked. The most important thing is, we'll tell them the truth when we are both ready. Trust each other to do the right thing."

"Sylvie, I trust you with my life."

"I know. You gave me this amazing gift, and I'll do anything to make this work. To protect us all."

Knowing that the girls would not be identical twins had sealed the deal.

"It also gives us enough breathing space. We'd probably need it, you know."

Sylvie had nodded in agreement but felt tortured by the idea of being without the woman who helped her navigate life as a young adult. She struggled to begin such a new chapter without Ava right by her side.

"How will I cope without you?"

"It's the price we have to pay. And it's a few months; then little by little ..."

Ava's voice faded away as Sylvie looked at her with wet eyes. She'd just always been there for her, through thick and thin. In a funny sort of way, she was still doing so. Another life-changing plan had hatched that day, though, with no one of them being the wiser.

Chapter 26

Glasgow 2010

Spending time with Michael helped Sylvie sharpen her instinct. She was getting better at picking the right moment to make a request; sedating him with his favourite Merlot — warmed gently to room temperature, of course — gave her the best chance of a positive outcome.

"Josie wants me to take her to the ice rink tomorrow. They're doing a free trial for skating lessons, and she's desperate to try it out."

"Is this a question or a statement?"

"This is a question, Michael. Please, can I take our daughter for a skating trial tomorrow after school?"

"Do you have a bit more information for me — like, who is the teacher, who else is going? Basic knowledge a responsible parent would ask."

Deep breaths, she thought, even if he could reduce her to a meek shadow with a few words. *Just get through this, for Josie's sake.*

"Well, it's the coach who was brought in last year by the local council, and — as far as I know — there will be at least ten other girls from Josie's school, too."

"And will this interfere with her homework?"

"We will work on that when we get home. She has promised me that, Michael."

"Oh, so you two already discussed this before you came to me?"

Schoolgirl error, that was. By some miracle, though, she seemed to have survived the grilling.

"I suppose a one-off trial won't hurt. I doubt she'll show much promise or staying power anyway — that girl's head is always going in a million different directions."

Sylvie knew better than to pick on the narrative he created about everyone else. "Is that a yes, then?"

"It's not a no, is it?"

Sweet victory.

The next day, they arrived at the ice rink fifteen minutes in advance, both Sylvie and Josie savouring every moment of freedom they carved out for themselves. Josie was already wrestling with her skates as they perched on the wooden benches positioned in the changing room. Something about the bristling temperature of an ice rink set Sylvie up for an adventure, and she was transported back to a time when she and Ava would meet up there, spend their pocket money on sweets, and mess around on the ice until one of them got too cold.

"Sylvie?"

Turning around, Sylvie found herself looking straight into a pair of eyes that she would never forget.

"...Ben?"

Ben was a friend from her school days, the boy she watched from afar, too out of reach. He was a quiet boy, the first one to truly turn Sylvie's head. Handsome, but in a soft, unconventional way, with his silken blond hair hanging over his eyes. It must have been years since Sylvie last saw him, and here he was again, standing in front of her on an ice rink in Glasgow.

He'd changed, but not much. His eyes were framed by a pair of glasses, trendy yet middle-aged appropriate. The laughter lines were deeper than she remembered, and his hair had receded around his temple; still, he stirred something within her, leaving her at a loss for words.

"Of all the places to bump into you!" Ben said, cutting through the awkward silence.

"Ben! Gosh, it's great to... are you taking to the ice yourself or —"

"Dad! Come *on*!"

"Robbie, hang on, son. Dad's just met a friend. Come and say hi."

"Hi! Can we go now?"

Ben looked embarrassed at his son's lack of manners, but Sylvie was too transfixed by this man to notice. Her own child did, though.

"Mum?"

"Oh, goodness! Josie, darling, this is Ben. Mummy's friend."

"Hi, Ben. I'm going skating. Are you going too?"

Ben's face lit up.

"It's lovely to meet you, Josie. I'm just here to watch my son, and he's getting very impatient—unlike you—so I better take him to class. Maybe your mum and I can watch you both together? You might be the next Torvill and Dean!"

"Torvill and who?"

"Josie!" Sylvie looked at her in mock disgust. "You want to skate and don't know who Torvill and Dean are? One of the greatest figure skating couples of all time."

"Oh, I know, Mummy! Jayne Torvill, the judge on Dancing on Ice? I didn't realise she used to be a skater herself!"

It was a brutal but entertaining reminder of their age bracket, and it made Sylvie feel connected to Ben. Her heart was beating just a little too fast as he walked his son towards a huddle of excited children. Robbie's age was around six or seven, she guessed, but his height made him appear closer to Josie's age. He already had his dad's subtle confidence and showed no signs of being overwhelmed by all the surrounding strangers. Ben looked relieved by something and Sylvie noticed his shoulders relaxing as he turned toward her again.

"Thank God there are some other boys. I had visions of him getting picked on like Billy Elliot on ice, but he was desperate to come today. Sees it as his first step towards Ice Hockey stardom after our trip to Canada last year."

Sylvie laughed while Josie followed some girls she knew from school. She wanted to relax and enjoy Ben's company. Why shouldn't she, after all? Escaping her own awkwardness was hard, however, and she stumbled over her words.

"It's Robbie, is it?"

"...Sorry, what?"

The music echoing around the rink as the class started up added another obstacle to their conversation.

"Your son, I mean. Robbie, is it?"

Ben nodded. He had that look of part pride, part despair so common among parents who watched their children play.

"That's right, after Robert the Bruce. Wife hated it, but there we go... I won that one!"

"He's very like you, Ben. "

"Poor sod, eh?" he said. "And your daughter, Josie, how old is she?"

"She's ten years old, as she keeps reminding me. Not sure where the years go?"

It was the benign chat you'd expect from two acquaintances who bump into each other at a school fayre, nothing more. She wanted to sit next to a man who didn't make her feel inadequate or scared.

"Where do they go, indeed." He looked a little uncomfortable. "I'd heard you had moved away. To London? Think I saw it in some Facebook group or something?"

"I did."

She was unsure if the stilted response was shorthand for
'don't want to go there, move on, please.'

"Well, it's great to see you anyw—"

"We split up."

"Sorry, what?"

"Julie and I. Robbie's mum and I split up about two years
ago."

"I'm… I'm sorry to hear that, Ben."

"Don't be. We were a ridiculous match. She had a lot of
demands and I only ever met a couple of them. On a good
day. With the wind going in the right direction."

In that very instant, Sylvie saw the sadness in his eyes and
hated Julie for making him feel like that. Inadequate. Faced
with her domestic horror show, she knew he was anything
but.

Time drifted away. This was the best life had been for a long
time, with her daughter happily pounding on the ice with her
skates and a man she didn't really know talking to her. What
was it she was feeling? Lust? Comfort? Whatever it was, she
felt drawn to him.

"And you, Sylvie, has married life been more successful for
you?"

Sylvie smiled. "I think so? Depends on your definition of
success, I suppose."

Ben looked unsettled by her response but said nothing, giving
her time to open up.

"Well, you know me, Ben. I need that strong arm now and then, don't I? Always was a bit of a daydreamer, and he doesn't have that problem. Very focused," she said, fiddling with the buttons on her jacket as she spoke. Ben watched her, seeming confused and concerned.

"Strong arm? What do you mean?"

"Mum! *Mum*! Did you see that? I went backward! Did you see it?"

"Wow, my darling, yes I did, but please do it again so I can pay proper attention."

"....Sylvie?" Ben said.

"Oh, ignore me. Let's watch our children. It's more fun than talking about marriage."

Josie wasn't quite able to re-enact the backward skate for Sylvie that day, but it planted the perfect seed for a return visit to the rink. Aware that this was dependent on getting the nod from the coach that she had some basic ability, Sylvie was delighted to be told her daughter would be welcome back to class. Ben was given the same news with the caveat that Robbie tries to focus on listening as much as increasing his speed on the ice next time.

"That's my boy," Ben joked as they left.

As the two families parted ways, Sylvie hovered by the door of her new Mercedes, feeling self-conscious in front of this man. Exposed. The life made of expensive cars and designer clothes was so distant from her old one, when they attended the same school.

"It was really lovely to see you, Sylvie. You're looking good."

Her heart fluttered, and she watched Ben head off with his son, ruffling his hair. Her time was up, though. The clock was ticking down, reminding her that she was expected back home, in a life that was hers to navigate.

Chapter 27

AVA

Edinburgh, 2010

Two weeks after Catherine's appearance on prime-time TV, Ava's self-loathing reached new heights. Her cheap stunt had failed, and she ached from knowing her daughter had laid her soul bare for nothing. Not so much as a text message from Sylvie. Besides, Catherine's popularity at school was already on the wane, and she was lonely again. At home, she disappeared into her own world, filling pages of her sketchbooks with beautiful, painful images.

"Sean, it's all been for nothing. I feel like an evil cow for putting her through that. Why didn't you stop me?"

Sean stared at her for less than two seconds before she shrank back, acknowledging the ridiculousness of her question.

"Sorry, I know. You tried to stop me."

"Ava, I learned a long time ago that trying to stop you when you have made up your mind is a waste of everyone's time." Ava was crestfallen, but she appreciated his choice not to rub her nose in it.

"You tried. You did what you could to bring these girls back together and give your best friend some means of escape. It's not a crime. Now, go and pick Catherine up, let's have a fun family tea together — minus the guilt."

"I love you, Sean Peterson. You know that?"

#

Once again, she was close to being late for school pick-up. Manoeuvring her car out of the parking spot was difficult, but she couldn't care less if the bumper ended up with another dent. The perks of having a low-value vehicle.

More hits than the Beatles, this one, Sean would often tease her. While she was busy with the car, the familiar sensation of being watched flooded her. Was her mind playing tricks on her with the memory of that day at the park? Was someone dashing across her rear-view mirror? Nothing seemed to confirm her suspicion, and she fought against the idea. Still, she felt it again, on her way back home.

I'm going mad. This is not helpful.

Turning around, Ava froze at the sight of a figure standing at the end of the road. The person was shrouded head to toe in a black coat, like something out of a low-budget crime drama.

I'm not going mad. I'm not, she thought, relieved. Apparently, it was better getting stalked than losing her mind.

"What are you doing, Mum?" Catherine said, but Ava had already swung the car into a parking space and got out, yelling at Catherine to stay put.

She rounded the corner and watched the figure slow down to pass a group of teenagers. It was all she needed to make out their silhouette; there wasn't a shadow of doubt about who she was looking at.

Chapter 28

SYLVIE

Glasgow 2010

Tuesday evenings became the highlight of their week. Josie
was convinced she had found her 'thing', the hobby that made
her tick. She worked hard and there was talk of a competition
which motivated her like never before. As for Sylvie, there
was the joy of Ben's company, a man who made her feel at
ease. There was something bittersweet being reminded of
everything Michael was not, the stark contrast between the
two.

One day, ten minutes into watching their children skate, Ben
turned towards Sylvie and looked her straight in the eyes.

"Are you happy, Sylvie?"

The question seemed a little forward, but she wasn't angry. It felt like an invitation to speak candidly, something she seldom did.

"I have my beautiful daughter, Ben. That's all I ever wanted."

"You know what I mean. Does he… does Michael make you happy, too?"

Sylvie felt ashamed. "How many people have everything they want? Truly?"

"It's not wanting, it's deserving. We all deserve to be happy."

"I'm happy here. Watching her and talking to you."

"If he doesn't make you happy, you don't need him in your life. You know that."

"There's Josie, too. He provides for her, everything she needs. We live well."

As soon as the words left her mouth, Sylvie felt dirty. The look on Ben's face spoke of mild disgust as well.

"Children need many things, but material wealth is pretty far down the list."

"Please stop patronising me. I'm doing my best with the cards I've been dealt."

"Sylvie, I'm sorry, I just — never mind."

"Michael and I couldn't have children of our own, so we adopted Josie."

"Wow. That must have been hard."

The understatement made her laugh. *You have no idea.*

"It was a friend. She was our… surrogate, I guess."

"That's pretty special Sylvie."

"So, you see, life is never straightforward, but I have my family now. And Michael, well, he's not perfect, but he's there, and Josie has two parents, like it should—oh, God, sorry," she said, realising her tactlessness. "I didn't mean. Obviously, sometimes things are better when… I mean, I'm sure you had good reasons. It's just, for me—"

"Don't worry, it's fine. And I'm not offended, trust me. We don't really know how we would react to a situation until we are in the thick of it, making decisions that affect your children."

Sylvie listened and felt the sincerity in his words. They cut through the fog of her own brain, and she saw her own life with a little more clarity. How did she get here? Tears welled in her eyes. She didn't want Josie to notice them and leaned into both her feelings and Ben, protected for the first time in years. Not controlled, coerced, or stifled, just protected and understood. It was good. Too good, so much she had to pull herself away.

"I'm sorry, Ben. You don't need this."

"Need what?"

"All this soul searching. It's easier if we just watch the kids, yeah?"

Cutting him off before he could reply, Sylvie stood and busied herself with her coat and gloves before picking up Josie, who was now taking off her skates. She was sitting next to a new friend, and Sylvie was so, so proud of her.

Shit, what have I done now? Sylvie inwardly chastised herself for allowing her emotions to show with Ben. No good can come of it. No good at all. The words circled in her brain, in a constant battle with the fleeting feeling of being whole again.

It was getting late. Sylvie hurried Josie along, knowing that Ben was waiting to say goodbye and that she couldn't face him. Her car was parked far from the front door, and she'd worked up a sweat by the time she began fumbling for her keys.

Then she saw him. Standing motionless next to the passenger side, dressed in his customary winter coat and suit, with shoes that had a military-standard shine on them.

"Shit, Michael, you scared me! What are you doing here?"

"Nice to see you, too."

"Are you checking up on us?"

"I'm not sure why you think I would need to do that. Can you enlighten me?"

Michael's specialty was asking uncomfortable questions. She knew they gave him an air of intellectual superiority over her.

"You don't. I just meant—never mind. Josie, look who's here," Sylvie said, faking enthusiasm for her daughter's sake.

"Daddy! Did you see me skate?"

"No, sweetheart, Daddy has just arrived. He has come straight from work just to surprise you. Well, actually, I did manage to catch some of the action from the back row—didn't want to disturb you or Mummy. She seemed rather deep in conversation. Would that have been the case, Mummy?"

"I, I was just chatting with—"

"Robbie's Dad! Robbie is a boy who comes skating, Daddy. He's *so* fast. Needs to, you know, listen more!" Josie delivered the last line with the mock secrecy that children carry off so well.

"Robbie's Dad, indeed? Looked like his dad was quite fast, too. I'm not sure I've heard you mention him when you tell me about these skating sessions, huh, Mummy?"

"I didn't think you'd be interested in conversations I'm having with other parents. I thought you were more interested in how our daughter is getting on with her coaching."

"Yes, you'd think we would both be most interested in that, wouldn't you?"

Could he have seen her being close to Ben? She had never talked to Michael about him, as he wouldn't tolerate it. She used to think his jealousy was sweet, but now she was just relieved he couldn't read her mind, know the way Ben made her feel. Her thoughts were her own. He could never control them.

"Let's go sweetie. Daddy will be hungry, and you have homework to do."

Then she heard Ben's voice from across the car park. "Sylvie! I think Josie left her hat?"

God, not now. Don't make me introduce you to him, please.

But something made Ben hold his ground. He moved slowly but confidently toward Sylvie and Michael, and she could tell he was assessing the situation closely.

"Hi. I'm Ben."

Shit.

"Ben, nice to meet you. I'm Sylvie's *husband*, Michael," he said, emphasizing the word as if to mark his territory.

"Michael, yes, I've heard… Sylvie has talked a lot about—"

"Thanks for the hat, Ben. We better dash now."

Sylvie was in a state of desperation, with sweat coating her forehead. He'd said enough, and she was now certain he knew, he *knew* and relished the thought of what would happen once they got home. Waiting for his wrath to unfold was the worst part of living with Michael.

He had taken Josie in his car, too, a way of preventing Sylvie from following her instinct and fleeing. She'd never leave without Josie, so she had no choice but to continue home, driving as slowly as possible past the gates of their driveway. The moment they parked, Josie jumped out of Michael's car and started shouting at her through the window.

"I'm *so* hungry, Mummy! What's for dinner?"

She was still in her seat, but she knew she had no choice. No options. After rubbing her eyes, she managed to smile before opening the door.

The hope that they could just have a normal evening was still alive as Sylvie went through the kitchen cupboards and the refrigerator. Tonight she'd make a buttered roast chicken crown with root vegetables and mashed potatoes; she'd do them the way Michael liked and everything might just be okay —

"Josie, sweetie," he said, with a calm tone that made her shudder. "Can you nip upstairs for a moment? Perhaps get started on your homework, and one of us will be up soon."

"But Daddy, I — "

"Go, *now*. And don't talk back."

Tears glistened in her eyes, but Josie disappeared upstairs, unaware of what was about to happen.

"Would you prefer parsnips or sweet potato chips?" Sylvie asked, wanting to deflect and redirect his attention. "The sweet potatoes looked so fresh, and I know Josie loves t — "

"Are you going to tell me what the hell you've been doing getting all cozy with that man behind my back?"

"Michael, don't. I didn't even know he would be there."

"Don't play the innocent with me, Sylvie. You've never been a great liar," he said. "I'll ask again. When were you planning to tell me the real reason for your trips to the ice rink, using our daughter as a prop to enable your liaisons?"

"For God's sake, calm down. Ben is an old school friend. I found out that his son was going to attend skating lessons too back when they started, and the only reason I didn't tell you was that I knew you would react like this!"

"But the problem is, I saw you. Both of you. You were almost in his arms at one point."

"Don't be overdramatic."

"Don't tell me what to do. Sounds like you were sharing all kinds of secrets with him, too."

"What? I just—" Nausea rose, and she thought she might be sick right there, on their bespoke granite kitchen worktops. "Michael, I'm sorry. It was just a friendly chat between old friends because I got upset talking about, er, how quickly children grow up."

"I wasn't born yesterday."

Just as she felt his rage reaching the boiling point, he stopped. He pulled back and visibly let himself calm down, silent and taking deep breaths. Sylvie stood, leaning on the worktop for balance, but not daring to speak.

"I had hoped we wouldn't reach this point, Sylvie."

"Point? What point?"

"When I have to remind you of what you could lose here."

Sylvie knew what Michael meant. This wasn't a new threat; she'd heard it before and it stood between them, dormant but present.

"You wouldn't... you can't. No, please, Michael. Not that."

"I have warned you. You need to understand that actions have consequences. Isn't that what we teach our daughter? Well, I say *our daughter,* but we both know the truth, don't we?"

"Michael, please. She's upstairs."

"It's not enough that you go behind my back to meet up with that woman. You also start getting cosy with a stranger who doesn't know how to keep his distance."

"It's not like that."

"Do they know?"

"Stop, please stop —"

" — Do they know what kind of woman you really are? Does Ava know the truth? Do they know the depths that you have fallen to?"

"No, Michael, they don't. And no good can come from it, least of all to our daughter, so please, please, I beg you to keep your voice down."

"Or what, she'll find out that her so-called mother is not her mother? Even though Ava lied about everything, *you* lied about why your body was defective. It had nothing to do with your big, brave, life-saving moment, did it? And I bet she didn't expect you to turn into a lunatic who tried to check out when things got tough."

"Stop, Michael... stop!"

"Because there was another, a longed-for child growing inside you when you swallowed those pills and washed them down with wine and vodka."

Sylvie fell silent. Devoid of energy to battle against him, she knew he still had further to go.

"We have a few little secrets, don't we? Just a word from me to let Ava know how you lied, how you killed your unborn child, and she may have reason to report you to the authorities."

Sylvie was moving towards him with her palms up, ready to either grab onto him or surrender. "Please, Michael, please, don't… it will ruin everything. Think about Josie—"

"Or should I just go to the authorities? It may have been a private adoption, but I bet someone would be interested in the welfare of a ten-year-old with a mother like you."

Exhausted, Sylvie sat in the corner of the kitchen.

"What do you want from me, Michael?"

"Ah, now, it appears I have got through to you at last. You see, there's no need for any of this to happen, if only you remember where your loyalties lie. You remember, don't you?"

Sylvie could only manage a nod, like a child desperate for it to end. He broke her without lifting a finger.

"Excellent. So, I suggest you find a way to either tell your daughter to look for an alternative skating class, or tell your school crush that he must look elsewhere for affection—and take his own son to a hobby more befitting of a man."

"Oh, God, you are cruel."

"Shall I take that as an agreement, or do we need to discuss this again?"

"I'll deal with it. I will. Just promise me you won't tell Josie?"

"The ball, as they say, is in your court, my dear."

Sylvie knew that the only thing Michael held dear was the control he had over her, and she could feel it eating her up inside, bit by bit, for the rest of her life.

Chapter 29

AVA

Edinburgh, 2010

Ava had seldom been more delighted to see her front
door. She'd endured the kind of day that felt as if the world
was whipping her up in some game of chance. The car broke
down five miles from civilization, and she dropped her phone
in the filthiest puddle she had ever seen; then a text from her
client informed her they would be 'shifting their business
priorities'. It was the kind of day that made her want to go
straight to bed, where she could enjoy *Netflix, Cadbury's
Heroes,* and a generous glass of *Baileys*.
She was peeling off her soggy jacket, seconds away from the
warm embrace of her home, when she felt a hand resting on
her shoulder.

"Jesus, what the fu—"

"Sorry, Ava. It's only me," Sylvie said. She had been hiding in her garden, it seemed, and was now standing next to Ava, her whole body shaking with tension.

"Shit, Sylvie, what are you trying to do?"

"I'm so sorry. I just needed to speak to you, and he can't find out."

"Is that arse still reading all your texts, then?"

"Ava. Please. Can I… can I come in?"

Ava opened her front door at once, before being struck by the domestic chaos within. It was a world away from Sylvie's picture-perfect home. Ava's was filled with the smells and evidence of its inhabitants, from home cooking to living a little too close together.

In a move out of the ordinary, it was Sylvie who spoke first while Ava put the kettle on and scrambled around for a pack of biscuits.

"I saw you both on TV."

Throughout their whole friendship, Ava couldn't remember another time when Sylvie looked at her with such sadness and disappointment in her eyes. It wasn't her style. "That was a cruel stunt. Pretty low, I thought."

"Fair cop. You're right—it was. I was desperate, and I didn't know how to get your attention. If it's any consolation, I felt like shit about it for... well, still do, really. Is that what you came here to tell me?"

"Ava, you don't understand," Sylvie said. Her eyes were full of tears as she perched on one of Ava's plastic chairs. "I'm so, so scared of him. I I what to do."

"Shit, Sylv. What's he done now?"

"He threatened me. You see, he knows too much. I'm so ashamed."

"What do you mean? What are you ashamed of?"

Silence. It hung in the air between them, like a poisonous odour.

"Sylvie? Talk to me."

"I'm not sure I can, Ava. I couldn't bear for you to hate me."

"What are you talking about? We've been through everything. I could never hate you."

"But I've got so much to lose now."

"Look, honey, I'm guessing you didn't sneak out of Fort Knox and come all this way just for my slightly stale chocolate hobnobs. Whatever it is, you need to tell me. I'm still your friend, no matter what life has thrown at us over the years. I want to help you. We can work this out."

Ava sensed a wave of calmness enveloping her friend upon hearing those words. Sylvie took a long breath before starting to speak.

"I was in a dark place. It was years ago, Josie was almost three and, you know, the shiny surface Michael uses to lure you in? It had long since rubbed off. He'd already chipped at my confidence and independence, moulding me into what he needed: a robotic servant he could exploit to feel important," she said. "I didn't have a job or anything of my own. He had ruined my dreams of opening a French restaurant—remember those dreams, Ava?"

Ava did, and her heart broke a little more at the memory of Sylvie's face lighting up when she spoke about the food she would serve in her little corner of France. The candles in old wine bottles with wax dripping down from the sides, and the handwritten 'Plat du jour' on a chalkboard outside.

"I had already cut contact with all my friends. All I had was Josie, and I love that child with all my heart, don't get me wrong, but I had nothing else and I spiralled down. I was lonely, sad, with Michael controlling me better and better."

"Sylvie, you are scaring me," Ava said, interrupting her monologue. She has probably waited years to let go, and Ava feared the punchline that was to come.

"I had an accident one day, a silly fall when I was up a ladder, but it hurt—a lot. I needed some serious painkillers to get about, and they helped. Really helped. That was the problem." Sylvie stared at her fingers.

"I know it sounds silly, but the painkillers became a support, a friend I didn't want to let go. They made me stronger and able to cope, so I kept taking them after the doctor stopped prescribing them. It's amazing what you can find on the internet. Problem was, they didn't seem to work so well after a while, and I was getting panic attacks and was in pain again. Such a predictable story; you must think I'm an idiot."

"Sylvie, I live a very imperfect life and I know that stuff like this happens to good people. Just please, tell me you got help."

"Well, I did, but not soon enough."

"What does that mean?"

"I was lost in my world one night. Michael had been cruel that morning; he's always delightful to me in front of her, of course, but when she was out of earshot, he told me I was a worthless junkie who was lucky to have them in her life. He set his expectations for the day and told me he would be home at half past six for dinner."

Ava couldn't believe what she was hearing. "This is the man that is co-parenting your daughter, Sylvie?" she asked, aware of how hard she sounded. Still, she handed Josie to her care all those years ago.

"I stared from my bedroom window all day before picking up Josie from preschool, cooking his meal, and attempting to tackle my chores. I felt like something had died inside me, though, like I had nothing else worth offering to anyone. So I waited until after dinner, went upstairs to run a bath, and swallowed my entire supply of pills in one move."

That was the same woman who had dragged her out of the water, her once fearless friend spilling her secrets. Horror raced through her mind, turning her blood into ice.

"What an utter coward. I just wanted to feel in control, even for a moment."

Why was I not there to save you?

"But I'm still here. Not that I cared at the time. The damage was done," she said. "When I woke up in hospital, the doctor told me I'd lost the baby. The baby. The baby was gone, and it was all my own fault."

Ava let the words sink in and considered them before speaking. "You were pregnant?"

Sylvie nodded, revealing years of pain.

"I didn't even know. Ten weeks. The miracle I thought would never happen."

The silence between them lasted for seconds but felt like a lifetime. Ava now understood what Michael held over her, and noticed how she was breathing with a little more ease.

"Sylvie, my... I don't know what —"

"That's not all."

Forcing herself to look up and make eye contact with her best friend, Ava watched as Sylvie appeared to search for the words she needed.

"Michael's controlling behaviour started much earlier."

"I get it. Remember, I knew him too. Even if it was a long time ago. He was already a prick back then, and I'm sorry to be so blunt."

"Stop, I need to get this out. The accident, when you were in the water and I saved you, my injury. It didn't… it wasn't the reason I couldn't have children."

"What are you saying?"

"I'm saying that we made it up. We lied to you when we told you I was infertile because of my injuries. It wasn't true."

Ava opened her mouth to speak, but nothing came out. All she could manage was a shake of her head.

"The adoption was based on a lie, and I could never tell you," Sylvie said.

"—What   ?"

"I'm so, so sorry."

There was nothing to say. Ava sat there, motionless and silent and thinking back to what she offered that day. When the words eventually came to her, they were all that seemed worth saying in a moment like that.

"You need to leave this man."

Ava held on to her friend tight that evening. Even why the crying had stopped and there was nothing left to say. No more secrets to offload. That was her moment. That was when Ava looked in to her best friend's eyes and told her that she would help her bring this man down.

Chapter 30

AVA

Edinburgh, 2010

Ava told Sean every miserable detail that night. They sat on the porch, sharing a bottle of cheap Chardonnay and drinking away anger and tears. Watching her husband listen to Sylvie's story, Ava fell a little more in love with him. She'd been so lucky, and maybe it was life's weird way of balancing out the good and the bad. Sylvie had such a blissful childhood compared to Ava, after all, and someone up there thought to even up the score.

"I know I should be full of anger, or guilt, or something else. We went ahead, and we both thought it was perfect, and it was all built on a lie."

"How could she be so brainwashed by him?" he asked. "I don't get that."

"I guess we never will understand what it feels like to have a man like Michael see your vulnerabilities and exploit them. Do you know what the weird thing is, though?"

"There's another weird thing?"

"I think I would have done the same, even without the fake injury tale. She was in so much pain, and if you have the power to help, you would, wouldn't you?"

"Not sure. They were twins. *Twins.*"

That night under the stars, Ava seemed to forget all her mundane concerns. None of them mattered. They were happy, and maybe it was time to accept that everything else must fall into place in due course.

"Are you coming to bed, Ava?"

"You head up. I'll be there soon."

She stayed long enough to finish the dregs of her wine, deep in thought. When she rose from her chair, something in her peripheral vision stopped her.

One too many Chardonnays, lady.

Then she heard his voice. It was low, but purposeful.

"We need to talk."

He was standing two feet from her back door. In her garden. For the first time in her life, Ava felt overwhelmed with fear and was too afraid to move or speak. The man who had stolen the very soul of her best friend and stood in the way of their e was there.

Ava tried to compose herself. She would not let him see he scared her.

"My husband is upstairs. What the hell are you doing on our property?"

"To address the first point," Michael said, still calm and unmoving. "I will be quick. Let's not disturb him. As for your complaint… oh, the irony! Do you remember when we last met?"

Ava's mask of bravery was dissolving in front of him. She shrank away from him, mindful of her daughter sleeping in the bedroom right above their heads.

"What do you want, Michael?"

"I want—" He cleared his throat. "No, forgive me, I *need* you to stay away from my family. It's very important to me, as I'm sure you understand, what with being a mother yourself. Nothing is more important than knowing your family is safe from, well, predators."

The veiled threat was not lost on Ava.

"I'm her best friend. Normal adults are free to contact their friends."

"Hm, but it's not just contact you want, is it?"

Michael cast his eye around her place. She knew that a loud scream would alert Sean, but she was determined to face him alone. She followed his gaze as it traced her small garden and the rear walls of her home.

"Basic existence you've carved out for yourselves here. Can't be much fun struggling for every penny; I bet you'd like to give your daughter something more."

Does this bastard think I want his money?

"No, you don't just want contact. You want to ingratiate yourself for your own selfish gains."

"I don't know what the hell you think you know about me, but you need to leave now."

"You need to be back in their lives, interfering and soothing your lingering guilt for the abhorrence you committed, giving your child away at birth." By now, he had Ava under his spell, hypnotised by his words. He must have chosen them with expertise, as he sounded skilled in tearing people down, piece by piece. "Couldn't bother with handling two at the same time, eh? I don't blame you, really; she is a bit of a handful— the one you punted in Sylvie's direction, I mean. A bit too spirited, but don't worry, I'm working on that. Little by little, I'm letting Josie see that compliance leads to a happy life."

Ava felt every muscle in her body tighten but stood her ground, struck by how devoid of soul he looked.

"I had good practice with Sylvie. The odd transgression aside, I'm confident she learned her lesson. That and the progress with the child are the reason I need you to back off. It's in everyone's best interests, or things could turn out poorly for Sylvie. I doubt you want that if you are the genuine friend you keep saying you are."

Holding his gaze at him, Ava searched for the strength to refuse him the fear he craved.

You truly are a narcissistic horror show.

"She's told me about your lies and blackmail, you self-centred piece of shit. I know everything and you can't bully me into staying out of her life because she needs me. I'll help her see through this veil of shame."

"That's admirable, Ava, but everyone has the odd skeleton in their closet, and I have a talent for sniffing them out."

Ava's mind whirled at once through the memories of her own secrets and he inched closer to her so she could feel his breath on her face.

"You think you can threaten me, too."

"We all have something to lose. We are not so different, as we both have people we hold dear and want the best for Sylvie and Josie."

Michael's words burnt.

"You have no idea what you're talking about. There's a difference between protection and control, so please get the hell out before I call the police."

"Now, let's not get overdramatic. It is easy to uncover secrets, given the urge some people have to divulge everything on social media. You really should watch out, it's so vulgar."

The rants and photos of Catherine filled her Facebook page. *How could I be so naive?*

"I suggest you keep an extra eye on that child of yours."

The rage in Ava's heart was uncontrollable. She watched him leave, walking as if he had just popped by for a coffee. She held off until he was out of sight, then her knees buckled, and she fell to the ground. As she remained there, waiting to regain her composure, she understood the power Michael had over Sylvie. That night, sleep didn't come for hours. He had both threatened and shone a light on the things worth having.

Chapter 31

SYLVIE

Glasgow 2010

"Mum! There's someone at the door!"
"Yes, okay, Josie, I'm coming. Give me a chance."
Sylvie was ironing her husband's shirts; they had been lingering in the laundry basket for two days until he ridiculed her for messing up such basic chores. She swept stray hairs off her face as she opened the door. The face behind it seemed familiar, yet hard to place.

"Hi, I'm so sorry to bother you. It's Angie. My daughter Lara has skating lessons with your daughter, Josie? We just live down the street." The woman pointed in the road's direction. *I know what 'down the street' means*, she thought, unnerved. Still, she mustered her best fake smile and waited.

"Hope you don't mind me turning up like this. Josie told Lara which house you lived in, and that's why I'm here—gosh, sorry, I'm rabbiting on."

Be pleasant but brief, and then she might leave faster.

"No, no, of course, Angie. Nice to see you," she said. It felt like Angie was assessing her. "Would you like to, er, come in?"

"Thanks, but no. In a bit of a hurry, I'm afraid. I just wanted to pass this on; it's from Robbie's Dad, Ben. We were chatting last week, and he noticed you hadn't been there for a while. We thought you were sick or something. Anyway, I mentioned how close we live to each other, and he asked if I could drop this letter by."

Both women looked at the crisp white envelope in Angie's hands, and Sylvie felt a spark of jealousy. This woman— Lara's Mum—had taken her place, chatting up with Ben and enjoying the warmth of his personality.

"Thank you for bringing it to me. So kind of you."

Sylvie knew Angie was hovering, waiting for an explanation for their absence, so she tried to move things along without being rude. "Well, if you're sure I can't offer you a cup of tea, I'd better let you go."

"Yes, yes, of course. Sorry. No doubt see you at the rink again soon?"

She answered with an awkward half-nod before closing the door.

"Who was that, Mum?"

Ignoring her daughter's question, she tore open the envelope and walked to her lonely kitchen. Perhaps it was a welfare check from a concerned parent and nothing more, but it terrified and thrilled her, regardless.

Dear Sylvie,

It was so lovely to see you these past few weeks. The years have been kinder to you than to me. You must be so proud of Josie, who is a great girl and with your same spirit of adventure. Robbie said she was the first girl worth speaking to, which is praise enough from a boy his age!

I need to cut to the chase, as time is not on my side. I need you to know two things, both of which I was working up the courage to tell you in person.

Apparently, I have a chronic and life-threatening health condition. It's got a fancy name — a cardiomyopathy — and I need a heart transplant within the next six months. All pretty sad if I let myself dwell on it too much, so forgive me if I don't. We didn't know each other well at school, but I always watched you from afar. Always wanted to ask you out, but Michael got there first.

I'm told I'm a decent judge of character, and I can see you are trapped in a marriage that, at best, provided you with security and wealth, which no one would blame you for being drawn to. But, forgive me for this, he is bad news. He controls you and frightens you, and he can't truly love you or Josie. I'm sorry for being so direct; there's something about a terminal illness that sharpens the mind.

I can't offer you much in the way of help or beyond the next few months, but I think you deserve more, whatever our futures hold. I'm here if you want to talk. Number's on the back of this letter.

Ben.

While reading, she had slumped on the floor and now she sat there, her head hanging low and her fingers gripping at the letter.

"—Mum? What's wrong, Mum? Why are you not listening to me, you're scaring me!"

Josie's voice broke her out of her reverie. Sylvie rose to her feet, feeling as if they might not hold her weight.

"Gosh, sweetheart, I'm so sorry. Mummy's fine, just dizzy. I had to sit down."

"On the floor?"

"Ah, yes, good point. Silly me, yes?"

Lunch. She needed to prepare their lunch. She opened the fridge and started pulling food out at random, wanting and needing a distraction.

"Mum, I'm not five. I can see you're upset. What was in that letter? What happened?"

"Oh, my darling. Sit down and let me make you a sandwich, and then we can chat."

"I'm not hungry."

"Okay, okay. It was just a letter from Robbie's dad, Ben. Remember, from the ice rink?"

"Of course, I remember. I've been missing all my friends from skating since Dad put a stop to that."

"I know you do, honey; I know. Well, Ben wrote to tell me he's not been feeling well, that's all."

"Bit odd, don't you think? Would you tell him if you were sick?"

Sylvie knew what she was up against, but she went on, attempting to protect her daughter and respect her curiosity at the same time.

"So, I guess he wanted to check if we were okay. We were friends a long time ago, even before I met Daddy, and sometimes, you still care about old friends and want to check on them."

"So the letter was about you, not him?"

"Josie, I've told you what you need to know. Now I want us to talk about something else."

"Mum!" Josie looked hurt and angry.

"Enough, please."

"Talk about something else? How about how lonely I am now that I can't even go skating anymore? Shall we talk about that?"

"Josie, I—"

Before she could finish, Josie ran upstairs while Sylvie realised that, for once, the thought of someone else overshadowed her concern for her daughter.

Chapter 32

AVA

Edinburgh 2010

Ava knew she was stubborn. It was borne, perhaps, out of the memory of her mother's intense belief that nothing positive would come of her. For the first time in a long time, though, she knew that stubbornness had its place, but not at the expense of her family's safety.

Her dilemma was simple: it was either to tell her husband about Michael's latest move and fight on or back the hell off.

In the end, she went for a hybrid. She told him that he was right there, in their garden and when she saw the look of horror on Sean's face, she reassured him that all ties will be cut with Sylvie for their own daughter's sake.

"That bastard was here, and you didn't call me?"

"Sean, you were asleep. I had it under control."

"Did you? Some lunatic trespassed on our back garden, threatened you before disappearing into the sunset, and you feel that everything was under control?"

"Sean, I said it's fine. He wins. He's right. I have too much to lose by messing with an arsehole like him."

"He wins? I'm sorry, what did you say?"

"You heard me. I am not going anywhere near Sylvie or Josie again."

"You're kidding. You opened a huge can of worms and now you give up? What are you going to tell Catherine? Have you forgotten that trick on kids' telly?"

"Sean, stop it. I made a mistake. I'm so —"

"Sorry? No, you are not. You are way too far down this road and I, for one, am not going to let you. Do you think we can go back to our life as it was before *Ava the saviour* marched into town and decided to launch a grenade into our lives?"

Ava looked into Sean's eyes, unsure whether her husband was making fun of her or of the situation as a whole. "Sean? What are you saying?"

Silence. It went on for a long while before he chose to speak again.

"What I'm saying is that you — we — need to see this through."

"*We?*"

"Well, no offence, but it seems you could use a little help."

"None taken," she said. He had her back, and the beginning of a smile was unfurling on her face. "I'm sorry for messing this up."

"To be fair, you didn't know you were up against Scotland's Psychopath of the Year."

Ava rubbed her temples, wanting to soothe the tension. She was jealous of Sean's ability to keep calm and bring humour to life's blackest moments.

"How can you always do that, Sean?"

"Do what?"

"You would have every right to gloat or to be an angry git for what I've got us into, yet you always make everything better."

Sean shrugged. "Maybe I know you were just trying to help and, despite my better judgment, I love you very much."

"Well, that's all very gallant, my knight in shining armour, but what do you suggest we do here? Joking aside, my family is way too precious to mess around with this devious shit."

"Ah, yes, but the good news is, I'm convinced he's not as clever as he thinks he is. These arrogant types get tripped by their own ego at some point."

By now, Ava was hanging on his every word. He, of course, noticed.

"Don't look at me like that. I hope you didn't think I had an instant solution for this problem."

"Well, yes?"

"Anything I could come up with wouldn't stand a chance against any plan of yours."

"Is that supposed to be a compliment?"

"Call it a motivational speech. Look, Ava, I just know a couple of things. First, you are always saying we must defeat our enemy head-on and when they least expect it."

"Do I? How profound. What about the second thing?"

"You have to remember that whatever you decide, I'm there for you. A bit like your wingman."

"Ah, I see. You're the Goose to my Maverick. The Scrappy to my Scooby Doo."

"Jeez, I just know you are the strongest person I've ever met. Just promise me there will be no more talk of throwing in the towel and letting that waste of oxygen win."

Ava gave him a bright smile, the one that said *it's us against the world, nothing will bring us down.*

To any outsider, it would have seemed an odd time to be picked up and taken to bed, but for Ava, it was perfect. She knew they were bound to each other just as much as they had been the day they got married.

The next morning, the sound of Catherine pacing around the kitchen and some awful drama unfolding on *Nickelodeon* woke her up. Ava made it there as well after putting on her dressing gown and getting their milk.

"Morning, Mum."

"Morning, sweetheart." She kissed Catherine on the top of her head and went to grab the kettle. "What's that?"

There was a card lying next to Catherine's breakfast bowl.

"Oh? Oh, yes, that was in the post. It's nothing, just a silly card from a friend."

"What friend?"

She should be happy to hear that her daughter was getting a gift, but there was something in her tone that made her uneasy. "Very secretive and so early in the day!"

"Oh, Mum, don't be silly! A girl is allowed to keep a secret, surely?"

Catherine popped her bowl in the dishwasher, kissed Ava on the cheek, and made it to the door, the card inside her pocket already.

"I'm walking to school again with Becca, Mum. You can stay in that dressing gown a bit longer. Love you."

"Love you too, darling."

Chapter 33

Glasgow 2010

"I'm going out after work tonight. You may as well eat early with Josie. I'll be late."

Michael's tone was short and to the point, and Sylvie welcomed it. His belligerent moods would drain the life out of her, while on days like these, she could just watch him walk out.

Then she would have to face hours of loneliness and boredom, punctuated by preparing Josie for school and feeding her. Not today, though. Something else burning in her heart; Ava and Ben's words had been playing on repeat in her mind.

You have to leave this man.

He's bad news. You deserve better.

Were they just the desperate ramblings of a man facing his own mortality and a jealous friend? The thought that she could elicit such raw emotions was too much for her to comprehend after Michael had sapped at her self-worth. Still, from somewhere deep inside, she allowed Ben's words to reach her.

Sod you, Michael.

She knew she didn't have long and needed to make sure she was back before Josie got home. First, she washed every dish, wiped every crumb from the worktops, and hid the clothes she still had to iron in the back of her linen cupboard. Then she grabbed a green knee-length dress from Hobbs and threw some makeup in her handbag, stopping only to lean on the pillars of her front door; some physical support was what she needed.

You can do this.

Sylvie had memorised the address, as she couldn't take the risk of Michael finding it—because he would. He made sure that Sylvie had no hiding place for personal items.

When she reached his house, the light in the front room was on.

Keep your nerve, a voice in her head told her while she sat in the driver's seat. It was the same voice that compelled her to jump into the water all those years ago — her moral compass, maybe, or a primal instinct. The label didn't matter; it just drove her toward what was important. Before she knew it, she was ringing his doorbell.

Jump in that water. Don't think too much. It's now or never.

Ben opened the door with the same enthusiasm as someone who was about to greet a salesperson or the gas meter man; then he froze. Sylvie watched as pink coloured his neck and cheeks.

"Sylvie."

"State the obvious, yes?" she answered, and it came out a bit harsh because of nerves. "Sorry. Gosh, sorry. I didn't mean that. I haven't thought… maybe I shouldn't be here."

He looked at her and she let herself believe that he'd just come to life.

"Please, come in."

Before doing so, she checked her surroundings. It was an instinctive move. Always watching her back, looking for her minder or wondering if she left any trace behind. She had left her mobile phone in the kitchen, as she knew he had installed something on it that let him trace her at all times.

Ben's home was cozy and functional, fit for a single father and his son. The front porch was littered with football boots and training shoes caked in mud, while a large TV sat in their living room with wires hanging below. Acutely aware of the clock ticking, Sylvie pulled herself back to focus on why she was there and let instinct guide her, cutting to the chase.

"Ben, your letter. I got your letter."

Shame darkened his face, and Sylvie regretted being so forward.

"Ah, yes, on reflection, I'd say that was not the kindest way to deliver the news. My options were limited, and I got the impression that your husband wouldn't take kindly to a visit from another man."

"I'm so sorry."

"About what? My illness isn't your fault."

"I don't know what to say."

Shit, what was I thinking? Turning up without having decided what to say is not your smartest move.

"Do you mind if I sit down?" he said. Colour was already draining from his face. "It's been a tough night, so not the best on my feet today, sorry."

It felt natural to sit with him, close to him.

"Your heart. What are the chances?"

"What, so you know if I'm worth investing time?"

His words were so bleak they crushed her spirit. He noticed right away, though Sylvie as he took a long deep breath before continuing.

"Sorry, that was wrong. I guess I've become blunt lately. My fate is in the hands of the organ donor register. If they find me a heart in the next six months, then I've got a pretty decent chance. If not, well, the year ahead is not looking good. I'm pretty high on the waitlist anyway, so let's look at the bright side."

All Sylvie could do was listen, letting the words sink in and found herself picking some stray hairs off her trousers to buy herself time before speaking again.

"Ben, why did you say that other stuff about me? About Michael?"

"I know I went too far. And if I thought for a second that you were happy, safe and living the life you deserve, I swear I wouldn't have written that letter. But, you are none of these things. I was worried about you. There was real fear on your face when he arrived that day."

"I'm in too deep, and you can't help me. He's—"

"He's what?"

"It's hard to explain, but he provides for us and I can't take that away from Josie. Besides, he would follow us. Hunt us down, and then God knows what. I can't take that risk."

"You have to."

"Oh, Ben, why do you even care? It's not like we were close."

"I was invisible to you. You were into spending time with Ava and impressed by Michael. Trust me, though, I cared about you."

Sylvie reached out to touch Ben's leg, then he lifted her hand to his cheek. Silence filled the air between them until she leaned in and kissed him. It was soft, gentle, and cautious; almost afraid. She pulled away after a moment and looked down in shame, but he lifted her head and took her in his arms before kissing her once more. This time it lasted longer, even if Sylvie pulled away again.

"Ben, I came here because I needed to be around someone who made me feel safe, but—"

"—I'm glad you did—"

"—But I don't want to drag you into my nightmare."

"I have nothing to lose, don't you get that?"

"Our children. We both have children, and he's dangerous. If he knew I was here…"

"Sylvie, why do you think you can't provide for Josie by yourself?"

"Because of security. Familiarity. She's used to her life, and so am I. Better the devil you know, as they say."

Sylvie felt vulnerable and, above all, exposed.

"I must go, Ben. I shouldn't have come."

"Yes, you should. Please let me help. I promise I won't try to—we can be friends. I get that."

By now, Sylvie was already heading for the door, even if she could still taste him and feel the burn of his stubble. She had been powerless against his hands on her back or the touch of his   fingers combing through her hair.

Minutes later, Sylvie was driving home, drunk on adrenaline and fear. It felt different from the one she was used to, and she wondered if she was falling for a dying man or running from a dangerous one.

She made it home with an hour to spare. Trying to calm down by herself would be futile. There was only one person whose voice she needed to hear.

Ava answered within the first two rings.

"Sylvie?"

"Ava, I need you. I'm in such a mess and I don't know how to—"

"Calm down. What's wrong? What happened? Has that arse hurt you?"

"No, that's not it. It's Ben. Do you remember Ben Ritchie from high school?"

"Er, I guess… floppy blonde fringe. A bit moody. What the heck has he got to do with anything?"

"I've been seeing him at Josie's ice-skating practice. He's… Ava, he's dying. Or, he might die if he doesn't get a heart transplant soon."

"Shit, that's awful. "

"That's not all. He, I mean, we—he kissed me. No, I kissed him. He said he wanted to help me leave Michael… it was so stupid… I don't know what I was thinking. What am I going to do?"

"Sylvie. Did you want to kiss him?" Ava was always direct. It was one of the things that made her both endearing and infuriating.

"That's not the point. It's a mess, I… when he told me he was dying, it changed something inside me. It made me want to fight. He reminded me of the person I used to be."

"I know that person, Sylvie. She saved my life, remember?"

"Yes, but what about Josie? Who knows what Michael would do to us if he found out about any of this."

Ava listened to the silence between them for a moment before responding.

"The way I see it—the way Sean and I both see it—is that you are married to a monster who has no interest in your happiness or your daughter's."

"But it's not just about me. As a mother, you should understand that, too."

"Yes, I do. And, as a mother, I'm asking you what Josie would lose without Michael in her life. Forget the fancy house, the school, and all that jazz. What would she miss that actually matters?"

"Ava, I'm scared of struggling to pay the bills. I've seen others battle with that and it looks exhausting and heart-breaking and just too hard. You, of all people, should get that."

"Tell me about the kiss. Was it, you know, delicious?" Ava asked, and Sylvie noticed that she chose to ignore her last words.

"Oh, it was like we were twenty-something again. I forgot what it feels like to kiss someone you really fancy. But, the funny thing is… I think that's all I need. I don't think I need a man in my life at all. I just need the right life."

As the words came from her mouth, Sylvie seemed to understand herself more. She knew this was her moment to find the truth, no matter how painful it felt.

"Ava, I need to ask you something and you won't like it." Hearing the awkward silence down the line, Sylvie knew she had to ask the question that was niggling at the back of her mind.

"The way you are trying to convince me to leave Michael, is it because we lied to you? Do you feel, I mean, would you feel as strongly about it if Catherine and Josie weren't — what I mean is — "

"What you mean is, do I care about what's best for you?" Ava asked, probably fed up by Sylvie's hesitation.

"Yes."

"Are you asking if I just want to protect Josie because I gave birth to her?"

"Yes, Ava."

"I don't know. What I do know is that I can't stand by, I can't watch you turn away from happiness, because I'm your best friend. You saved me once. I owe you everything."

"No. You repaid that debt the minute you handed her to me." Sylvie had to face the question hanging in the air. "What if he carries out his threat, though?"

A silence hung in the air and Sylvie imagined Ava struggling for answers.

"He knows everything," Sylvie said. "If he tells Josie, it could devastate her. She could have had a brother or sister if I didn't miscarry, and I lied to get a baby, separating her from her soulmate."

"These girls can still have a future together, but we need to tell them the truth before they find out — or, God forbid, before he tells them."

What ifs were torturing her. What if she stood up to him when he'd started isolating and gaslighting her? What if she had found the strength to leave his wealth and control sooner? She knew Michael wouldn't hesitate to sink as low as possible, and she needed to find a way out.

Chapter 34

AVA

Edinburgh 2010

There was something in Catherine's eyes that stopped Ava dead in her tracks.

"Catherine?"

No answer. Not even a pit stop in the kitchen for a snack or a drink to keep her going until dinner was ready.

"Catherine, what's wrong?" she repeated, but her daughter walked straight past her and up to her room. Instinct prompted Ava to drop everything and follow her, a move Catherine didn't seem to appreciate.

"Mum, leave me alone. Please."

"What on earth happened? I've just seen a missed call from the school. Is it your friends? Has someone said something to upset you?"

"Eh... yes, Mum, yes."

The hostility in Catherine's voice was something Ava had never heard before.

"You're worrying me."

"Leave me alone."

Taking a seat at the end of Catherine's bed, Ava spoke quietly but with resolution.

"Catherine, I'm not leaving until you've told me where you have been today."

At ten years old, Catherine was picking up some early teenage mannerisms, one of which was a sharp temper.

"I met a friend of yours today, Mum. And he told me some very interesting secrets about you."

"What friend? What are you talking about, Catherine?"

Ava could feel her hands begin to shake. She sat on her daughter's bed and rested them on her pink duvet cover to steady her nerves.

"*What* friend, Catherine?"

"Michael. His name was Michael."

No. Please no.

Ava began to pace around the room. She could hear Catherine continue to talk but was terrified to listen.

He sent me a letter and told me that he was one of your oldest friends and wanted to arrange a birthday surprise for you. He met me after school — that day that you thought I had gone home to Lucy's house. He knew all this stuff about you, Mum, so I knew it was safe.

"Jeezus, Catherine. Have I taught you nothing about safety?
You're almost eleven and..."

Ava stopped herself. It took all her strength, but she had to
keep Catherine talking.

"I know, Mum, I know. But he had all these fun ideas about
arranging a party and I just let him talk. But then, there was
something about him that made me scared to leave. I can't
describe it. I..."

"It's ok, sweetheart, it's ok. I know."

Ava reached out to Catherine and tried to hold her hand, but
she pulled away at once   .

 "Eventually, I told him I had to get home, and that's when he
said it."

"Said what, Catherine?"

"He said he wanted to tell me a few more secrets about my
mum."

"Talk to me, Catherine… what did this man say?"

"No, Mum. I can't. I—please just leave me alone."

Ava was sick with the terror of what was coming next when
her mobile phone began to vibrate on her lap, showing a new
message from an unknown number.

Two minutes later, the instant messenger notification lit up.
The sender was Michael. She felt violated by seeing his name
on her screen, but clicked on it, anyway.

—**Lovely to meet your daughter today. She's a smart cookie.
Tell me, does she get that from her father?**—

Dizziness engulfed Ava. *How the hell could I have let this
happen? And what has he said to her? Bastard. Bastard!*

A thin layer of sweat appeared on her skin and she struggled
to take a breath. She shouldn't answer, but she was helpless in
the face of her own anger.

—What the hell were you doing with my daughter, you arrogant prick? I'm calling the police—
She sent it before she could think twice. Then she waited for a reply.

—We were just having a lovely chat. She came by her own free will. Reminds me so much of Josie, but that's hardly surprising. Seems lonely though, lacking in the friend department. To be honest, I think she liked the attention—
Ava felt a thin layer of sweat covering her forehead and her hands shook wildly as she composed another text.

—Stay the hell away from her or I will have you arrested—
she wrote, and she wished her words could hurt him like punches.

—What the hell did you tell her?—

—Oh, keeping things close to her chest, is she? There comes a time, though; a coming of age?—
Ava heard enough. She threw her phone down and tried again to talk to Catherine, but she had clammed up and threatened to run away if she wasn't left alone, so she left her room and forced herself downstairs to think.

Sean. She should tell Sean, but she had no idea when he'd be home, and dialling his number only connected her to his voicemail. The text she sent right after was short and to the point.

—Sean, he met up with Catherine today in secret. I need you to do me that favour. We have got to take this shithead down.

Chapter 35

SYLVIE AND AVA

Glasgow 2010

SYLVIE

Josie had been helping her mother prepare dinner when she piped up with an odd question. Her daughter loved the quiet moments between the two of them and often chatted with ease given the opportunity.
"What is a gold-digger, Mum?"
Sylvie's attention was immediately aroused.
"A what?"

"Gold-digger. Does it mean something different to someone who finds gold in rivers, like in that Discovery program?"

"It can, yes. Why do you ask, my love?"

"I heard Daddy use that word on the phone."

On the surface, this wouldn't have alarmed Sylvie as she's heard him throw around similar accusations plenty. She knew he wore his wealth like a badge of honour and often dismissed as gold-diggers those who stood up to him.

"Sometimes, Josie, it can mean someone who is only interested in you because you have more money than them."

"Or more gold?"

"Yes, or more gold!"

"So, what would a gold-digging tart be, then?"

The knife Sylvie was using to cut cucumbers slipped and almost took off her forefinger.

"What did you say? No, I heard it. Please don't repeat it again. When did Daddy say this?"

"A while ago—maybe last month? Just thought about it now because I was looking at your pretty gold bracelet."

"Josie, what else did you hear?"

Sylvie hated herself for asking that, but she was also human, and she couldn't let this one go.

"I think he was talking to Daisy. You know, work-Daisy."

"I know Daisy, yes."

"He had that tone he gets when he's very busy. I remember him saying something like, *Just pay her to go away, the gold-digging tart*, and then something about the gold-digger being *fruitless, anyway*. I thought that was another funny word to describe a person. Did he mean a fruitless tart?"

"Yes, yes, I think he meant that."

Josie continued peeling her carrots, oblivious to the turmoil in her mother's head.

Sylvie had learned to accept that ignorance was bliss when it came to Michael. There was something liberating in turning a blind eye to his business deals; in public, she was content to smile and play the doting wife, letting her innocence shine and clean him of his sins, too.

This felt different, though. She sensed there was suffering behind all this — not infidelity, but something worse — and had a good idea where to look for answers.

"Josie, Mum's just going to clean Dad's office. You carry on down here, and watch your hands on that sharp peeler, please," she said before running upstairs.

Like so much of her husband's life, Michael's home office did not give up its secrets easily. Sylvie had found herself trying to find some paperwork once before — a guarantee for something electrical that stopped working- but gave up trying after finding every cabinet locked. She knew Michael scanned and filed paperwork away, hid keys in a safe, and protected his computer with a series of intricate passwords. Until now, Sylvie had little motivation to penetrate his system. She pulled out his antique leather desk chair and sat, for once feeling like the master and commander Michael pretended to be.

Think, Sylvie, think.

Michael had modelled his home office on what Sylvie remembers of his office in the city. It was one of the largest rooms of his firm, in an arrogant-looking building in the exclusive West End. Since being made senior partner, he wanted everyone to remember it. His name was listed everywhere, from the embossed brass signage at the front entrance to the pens and mugs that adorned both his office and the homes of his clients. He often reminded her that there was no shortage of wealthy individuals and landowners in Scotland who were willing to pay a premium for his 'exclusive' legal services.

As Sylvie looked around his ornate home desk, she saw even more evidence of his obsession with personalised items. Engraved brass pen holders, and a leather-trimmed writing pad at the centre of a desk which had little else on show. She knew anything important was hidden behind lock and key.

#

AVA

Sean Peterson had been working at *Business & Legal* for a number of months now.. Long enough to build some relationships — it was what he did well. Ava knew that Sean was a well-liked man. The popular guy in the office. It was one of the things she found irresistible from the first time she met him. There were many days when she questioned the value of picking up friends like collecting stamps. How many different people you need to drink a pint with or watch a football game, she would ask? Right now, though, she actually got it. She understood that, sometimes in life, it could be really useful to have favours to call on from people. She knew Sean was going to meet his editor, Pete, for a drink after work in order to get him on board with their plan. Pete was your classic business news hound. Rough around the edges, but had risen through the trenches of business journalism by being relentless when it came to corporate mischief. Sean assured her he wouldn't put up any obstacles, but she was desperate for an update and reached for her phone.

"Honey, it's me. How's it going? Is Pete up for it?"

"Hell yes, the interview is already set up. He's going to the tosser's house tonight. Couldn't have jumped at the chance of glory any faster, it looks like. He really is the classic, arrogant sod who's expecting some puff piece emblazoned over our front page next week."

"Thanks, Sean. I love you for this. We both do. I realise it's shaky ground."

"She's my daughter too, remember, Ava? I don't need to keep saying that, do I?"

In a brief respite from the anger that was cursing through her veins, Ava allowed herself to feel a little self-satisfied with the masterstroke, though. Then she remembered it all started with Sylvie and Josie's bravery. Despite everything, she had found the guts to share what she needed to. The seed of Michael's downfall was planted by the innocent words of a child. No one is untouchable, she told Ava. Not even Michael.

#

SYLVIE

She could feel his feathers puff out when he called her to say he would be late home for dinner.

"I've had a call from an editor, Sylvie."

"An editor?"

"Yes, Sylvie, an editor. You know, the people who are in charge of newspapers and magazines?"

"That sounds exciting," she said, aware that it was better to let his patronising sarcasm float through her. "What did he want?"

"It was the editor of Business & Legal, the magazine that features the great and good in Scottish Business and the Legal sector, you know?"

"Yes, Michael, I do."

She didn't know. Why would she care about such a publication in the short time she had returned to Scotland? Still, she refused to admit her ignorance.

"What is it that they want?"

"Apparently, they want to interview me for a piece in the magazine."

Sylvie imagined his chest expanding as he spoke.

"And you said?"

"I said I would be delighted, but they would have to come to the house tonight, as I'm busy for the rest of the week. The clients are literally queuing up—it appears there is still no end of Glaswegians in all kinds of trouble, needing me to bring some brains to their rescue."

Sylvie knew that Michael revelled in exerting his intellectual superiority on those around him. She sensed his ego would be stroked by the prospect of being featured in this magazine, following other illustrious businessmen.

Michael arrived home at around half past six, thirty minutes earlier than expected. He was even more preened and polished than normal, as if the smell of his cologne could be transferred through the pages of the magazine.

He reminded Sylvie not to disturb him for the duration of the interview, so, after bringing a freshly made pot of coffee, she closed the door behind her—almost. She had perfected the art of leaving the slightest gap between it and the doorframe unnoticeable from his side but wide enough for her to listen. She didn't often use this privilege as it was not a pleasant experience, but today was different. Ensuring that Josie was occupied upstairs, Sylvie hovered as close as she could, taking her shoes off and avoiding the floorboards that creaked the most.

"Wonderful to meet you, Mr Miller."

"Oh, delighted to have you. And do call me Michael. Welcome to my humble abode."

Sylvie had noticed that Pete brought along a cameraman, dressed in slightly ageing jeans and a rock band T-Shirt. "Can I pour you some coffee? My wife brews a fine pot of Colombian beans."

Patronising as ever, Sylvie thought, while bile rose in her stomach.

"Thanks, but no. Happy to crack on if you are?"

"Great, so let's get to the bit where you ask me those tricky questions, shall we?"

She heard the sound of leather creaking and knew that Michael would be adjusting his position for maximum presence in the room. Moments later, she heard a short click and faint whirring sound coming from the chair nearest the door.

"You don't mind if I record this, do you?"

"Of course not, no margin for misinterpretation this way, yes?!"

It was a subtle warning shot that Sylvie had heard before. She noticed that Pete was warming Michael up by asking lots of benign questions about his career path, work ethic and future ambitions. He relaxed him enough before he struck with full force.

"All very impressive, I'm sure. I wondered if we could chat about a slightly different topic."

"I'm sorry, I get so carried away when I talk about this company. The work we do here for our clients runs through my veins with a passion. What else can I tell you?"

"Interesting you mention passion, Michael. Would you describe yourself as a passionate man?"

The sound of Michael's chair moving again was all Sylvie could make out. The silence in the room was painful.

"I'm not sure I'm following?"

"Passionate. It's an interesting word. Is that how you felt about Agnes Rollo?"

Sylvie could feel her own pulse quickening and didn't know if it was excitement or utter terror.

"Or Maggie O'Hara?" Pete said, pressing him on. "Similar feelings of passion there? Or was it something else that motivated you? Greed perhaps? Entitlement?"

"I'm sorry, I have no idea where we are going with this."

"You don't? Oh, okay. Let me explain. So, I've heard that your squeaky-clean reputation may just be a little tarnished around the edges you see?"

Sylvie was shaking now, and she stepped back to steady herself, making contact with a loose section of flooring. Her heart stopped for a moment, but no movement came from within the office.

"I've spoken to Agnes and Maggie, you see. They had quite a lot to tell me. I think you may have underestimated them, Michael."

"I think it's time we wrapped this conversation up, instead. I thought you were a serious business publication. My mistake, obviously."

"Oh no, I would say your mistake was taking advantage of women who were in a vulnerable place to suit your own needs before dismissing them when they got a little bit too demanding. Agnes, for example. Remember offering her the world as encouragement to visit you after office hours when it suited you, then dismissing her when she got too impatient? Or what about Maggie, who was promised a promotion if she could keep her mouth shut about your extracurricular affairs but got shunted to the bottom of your list when she found a boyfriend who had her best interests at heart?"

Sylvie heard Michael stand up now and she began to retreat back down the hall, straining to make out their words.

"What's the matter?" Pete said. "Didn't expect these women to resurface after all this time? You should keep a closer eye on the news, you know. There's a bit of a groundswell of intolerance to men like you now. I Think the whole sexual exploitation approach to management is a bit last century."

"This interview is finished. Could you please leave my home so that I can get on with my day?"

Sylvie was back in her kitchen by the time she heard Michael walking Pete and his colleague to their door.

"Do you honestly think this unsubstantiated drivel is fit for the pages of a business magazine, if that's what you're threatening me with?"

"I don't care. As well as being an editor, I'm also a freelancer. I can sell it anywhere. Tabloids would love it. Oh, and there are others by the way. Agnes and Maggie gave us more names. They talk to each other, you see. Hadn't quite worked up the courage to make a formal complaint yet, but I guess that's where we could come in. Giving a voice to the gagged and bound, I guess you could say."

Michael moved towards Pete while Sylvie watched, until they were face to face. "I have no idea what game you think you are playing here or what these women have told you, but I would like to remind you that writing anything careless about myself or our firm could end badly for you. We are lawyers with considerable resources at our fingertips. Take it from me, the testimony of a few women who didn't like getting dumped is not going to go very far in a courtroom."

As they left, Pete and his valiant accomplice delivered their killer line.

"Oh, whoops, here's me thinking I stopped the tape recording earlier, but would you believe it, the little green light is still flashing. How careless of me! I am glad we picked up that last little gem from you, anyway. I know that threats have worked for you in the past. It's kind of what makes your kind tick but, trust me, I've been threatened by better shitheads than you in the past. If you decide you want to comment on these allegations, do let us know."

#

SYLVIE

As soon as the door closed, Sylvie could sense how wrath was burning inside her husband. He did not speak to her or Josie and went straight back to his office, closing the door behind him. She could still hear him swearing and slamming drawers shut.

It happened, she thought. Michael had dived headfirst into new territory — he lost control of things. Knowing it thrilled and terrified her in equal measure, but as she watched Josie doing her homework at the kitchen table, she told herself to stay calm. His next move would be unpredictable; hers would not. She would stand there while he unravelled under the pressure and became distracted. Protecting his reputation would be more important than keeping them on a tight leash.   And Sylvie would be ready to seize the moment. Her chance was now — when she knew he was looking the other way. Sylvie picked up her phone and let her fingers hover over Ava's number, before throwing it in her handbag and reaching for the overnight bag she had hidden at the back of her wardrobe. Pacing along the hall towards the kitchen, she entered it quietly and calmly asked Josie to get ready to leave as soon as possible.

But Sylvie knew Michael was not one for patience. The clock would be ticking and he would need to come up with a plan quickly.

Later on, as Sylvie approached the outskirts of Dundee, with a quiet and confused Josie by her side, she allowed herself to reminisce on the moment she discovered the hard drive he thought no one would ever see. Of course, it was in a drawer that was always locked. And the key…Sylvie knew it would be there somewhere. Where, though? Exploring the darkest corners of her husband's behaviours, she remembered the one domestic task that she was never allowed to do for him. Slice the lemons for his sparkling water.

Watch how this knife slices through it like a feather. It's like magic, don't you think?

He would insist Sylvie watched him and heard the words which were both hypnotic and deeply menacing. And that's where she had found it one day. A small, rather uninteresting looking key. At the time, she didn't know what it was for but guessed that it would become clear one day. And that day was now.

Sylvie still knew the way to Ava's house so well and was pulling on to her street when the thought hit her like a wall of fire.

She didn't return the knife box back to the right cupboard.

Chapter 36

AVA

Edinburgh, 2010

Ava had waited a full hour before going back to Catherine's room. At first, no answer came forth after she knocked, and that terrified her; when she pushed the door open as gently as she could, she saw Catherine was curled up under the duvet. Her breathing was the only thing that broke the silence, and it reminded Ava of the times she spent checking on her when Catherine was a baby.

Catherine's face was still red. She looked drained and was staring at something — Ava couldn't make out what it was, but she thought they were photos.

"Can I join you?"

Silence. Not an outright no, however, so Ava sat at the end of her bed. The conversation they were about to have petrified her, and yet she knew she had no choice.

"Catherine. Talk to me, please. Tell me what's happened."

"I don't think I can."

"I'm your mum. I love you more than anything, and you can tell me whatever you want."

"Really?"

"Of course."

"Do you tell me everything, Mum?"

Ava was always astounded by the maturity of her daughter's language. She was ten   years-old, but sounded as if she was going on sixteen at times.

"I don't understand what you mean, my love."

"*Everything*. Do you tell me everything?"

"Catherine, what happened today?"

Her head dipped low.

"Talk to me."

Fight the rage, Ava, fight it. Your daughter needs your support more.

"Okay, honey. The man who met you. His name was Michael?"

Catherine's head rose a little. "Yes, he told me he was Josie's Dad."

"Tell me what happened."

"I can't, Mum. I just can't."

"You can and you must, because that's the only way I can help you."

"He's a liar. He told me lies, but he made me believe them."

Ava's heart felt like it was about to break. Watching the tears in her daughter's eyes, she imagined what Michael had said to her and wondered what mother allowed that to happen.

"Tell me he is a liar, Mum. Tell me!"

"Calm down, please. Calm down and talk to me. Michael is *not* my friend, I can tell you that much."

The doorbell broke through Catherine's sobs. She ignored it. Twice. Whoever it was would get the message.

"Did he tell you something about me? About our family?"

Catherine managed a nod, and Ava knew she had to speak up herself. "Look at me, Catherine. Please."

For the first time in their life, there was doubt in Catherine's eyes.

"Did he tell you something about when you were born? Did he tell you something about your sister, my love?"

Upon hearing that, Catherine made the slightest of nods.

"Sweetheart, what *exactly* did he say?"

A noise downstairs. Someone was in their house.

Ava shot to her feet and made for the top of the stairs, where she had a full view down to the front door but none of the rest of the house.

"Stay there, Catherine," she whispered as she followed the noise downstairs. The moment she saw the person standing at the bottom of the stairs, she recognized her at once.

"Sylvie?"

"I'm so sorry, I did ring, but there was no reply and your door was open."

Sylvie had the look of a lost soul; free at last, but still scared about any predator following them. Next to Sylvie stood Josie, looking for answers, too. Answers that Ava feared someone would have to give now.

"I'm so glad you came to us," Ava said, running down the stairs to give Josie the warmest of hugs. It was an instinctive gesture, one she couldn't or wouldn't ask permission for. Josie responded with warmth as well, and Ava relaxed a little in her embrace. Then she turned around in time to see Catherine. Her daughter stood in the doorway, watching them.

"Catherine!"

Josie's joy was so real and innocent, it was almost enough to cut through their unease and tension. Still, Catherine stood where she was, rooted to the spot.

"Catherine, sweetheart. Please, go back to your room and I will join you again as soon as I've got Sylvie and Josie something to drink."

"Can I join, too?" Josie asked.

"*No*," Ava said, before catching her tone. "I mean, sorry, of course, you can. We were having an important chat, so I need you to wait with your mum for a minute."

Sylvie held her daughter close and looked into Ava's eyes.

"Ava, God, I'm sorry to show up like this."

"No, don't be sorry. Stay where you are. I just have to talk to Catherine." Ava paused. "You're safe here, both of you. I mean it—I'm glad you came."

Ava tried to busy herself for a while by pouring a drink for Sylvie, but her hands were shaking as she lifted the glasses out of the cabinet. She sat them on the sofa, switched on a film for Josie, and then made her excuses to return to Catherine upstairs. No more than fifteen minutes had passed before she entered her bedroom, but it was empty. No Catherine. She searched the rest of their house within minutes. Still no Catherine. *Oh, God, no. Please, no.* Pulling Sylvie off the sofa and back out into the hall on her own, Ava clutched her friend in a panic.

"Sylvie, she knows."

"What? How much does she know?"

Josie was sitting nearby, and Ava spoke in a desperate whisper. "She knows about the past. Everything. He told her."

"Who told her? I don't understand!"

"Michael did. The bastard got hold of her and met her on his own."

"Shit. God, Ava, what can we do? Where's Catherine?"

"Has Catherine run away because we arrived?" Josie. She must have heard them, after all.

"No, sweetheart, no. She just got a fright earlier and I think she's gone somewhere to think about it on her own, but we must find her. Can you stay here with your mum while I look?"

Josie nodded. "Except…"

"Josie, not now. Let Ava go, she has to find Catherine."

"I know, Mum, but I just wanted to suggest that I go with her. Remember how she was so clever and found me that day at the park? Maybe I will be able to do the same for her?"

Both women looked at each other, unsure but motivated by desperation. There were no easy choices here. Sylvie resisted letting Josie out of her sight, but soon the women agreed to let her go.

"Come on then. You come with me, and Sylvie, you stay here in case she comes back home."

Chapter 37

AVA

Edinburgh, 2011

They began their search on foot. Ava told herself that
Catherine could have only gone so far, but logic and
rationality didn't stand a chance against the panic of a parent
in her situation.
Cover as much ground as possible within a mile radius from home.
Josie followed along beside her, silent and thinking, she
guessed.
"Ava?"
"Yes, Josie. Do you have an idea?"
"It's probably silly... let's just keep going your way."

Ava stopped and stared at Josie. "I trust you. What are you thinking? Please, tell me."

"It was just something Catherine said to me when we spent some time together. She said that sometimes, when she feels lost, she likes to look for answers by herself."

Ava felt crushed. It meant nothing, but she tried to keep her cool, anyway; after all, she was speaking to a child.

"Okay, honey, so what do you think she meant by that?"

"What's she upset about?"

"I can't tell you now, not yet, but sometimes you keep things from loved ones for their own sake, but..."

"But they find out, anyway?"

Josie's words revealed so much wisdom to Ava. She couldn't help letting a wave of pride wash over her.

"I think I might know what she's upset about," Josie said.

Ava was terrified of how this would play out, but something told her it was no longer in her gift to control.

"Josie. Please, tell me where you think Catherine may be."

"It's just... Well, I once heard my dad shout something odd to Mum. He said I would be better behaved if I were their own flesh and blood."

"Oh, sweetheart, let's not talk about this without your mum here. I can't—"

"I know what flesh and blood means. It means your real family, doesn't it?"

Ava couldn't speak. One child lost, and she was talking to the other, who was just as lost.

"I've noticed things, you see," Josie pressed on. "I've noticed how alike Catherine and I are, even though I've not seen her much. We've got the same silly habits, we both play with our hair when we are concentrating. We love art; I love looking at it, but Catherine loves making her own. We are of the same height, almost, we're left-handed, and we are *really* bad at throwing balls."

Stopping herself mid-stream, Josie lifted her eyes and seemed to search Ava's face for something.

"Ava, are we? Are you?"

Breaking the trance between them, Ava wiped the dampness from her eyes and shook her head, dismissing the words coming at her.

"We have to find her, Josie. If you care about Catherine like I know you do, help me find her. I promise your mum and I will answer all the questions you have, but we *must* find Catherine first."

Ava's lack of denial seemed to be enough to convince Josie. Maybe she believed that the answers she wanted were within reach. Josie took Ava by the hand.

"I think I know where she's gone," she said, leading her towards the forest at the back of the local park. "I've never been here before, but Catherine described it so well and she drew it in some of her pictures. One of the pictures she showed on that tv program."

Hidden behind some bushes, there was an abandoned shed. The park warden used it once to store gardening equipment, and — by the looks of things — snatch the odd tea break here and there.

"She told me she goes here sometimes when you and her dad think she's at a neighbour's house."

Ava didn't think her heart could break further, and yet. "I had no idea she was struggling so much."

"I hope she's not cross with me for telling you."

"Honey, don't. You have done nothing wrong, and neither has Catherine."

Now they were close enough to peek through the window. It was black with dirt, but Ava saw movement inside. Catherine. Catherine was there.

Oh, thank God.

Her daughter was taping drawings, sketches, and paintings to the walls of the shed, oblivious to their presence. Ava wanted to run in and hug her, but she forced herself to stand still and watch the collection. Some subjects she recognised, places they went as a family, flowers, and items Catherine had at home, drawn both in dark and light tones. One face appeared more often than anything else, though. It was the face of the girl standing next to her.

A branch cracking under Ava's feet broke Catherine's concentration, and she turned around.

"Oh, my darling," Ava said. "Come here!"

Catherine, still full of hurt and confusion, looked at her mother with tears in her eyes. Then moved into her embrace, as if searching for the same comfort she craved as a very young child.

Her gaze shifted to Josie. "Is it you? Are you my sister?"

Josie and Catherine looked at each other, and Ava knew it said more than any words ever could.

"Michael, he… he told me I had a twin sister. He told me that my mum gave her away when she was born because she couldn't look after both of us."

"What else did he say, Catherine?"

"Nothing. Nothing, but now I know. I know, Mum. It's Josie, isn't it? She is my twin."

It was now clear that Josie had worked it out for herself too. She could see it in her eyes. She realised it had probably taken until now for her to force these thoughts to the surface but, only now, in this desperate night, was she able to see them clearly. Perhaps it was the looks that Sylvie exchanged with Ava when they arrived. Had she heard the words they said to each other and eventually made sense of them? Perhaps the way Catherine looked at her when they arrived gave it away? All of that should have been enough for a bright young mind such as Josie's to figure it all out. But, of course, the most convincing evidence was in front of her eyes, emblazoned in chalk, paint and pencil across the walls of this forgotten building. Her sister's refuge where she came when life as one half of a pair that should never have been separated became too much to bear.

Chapter 38

AVA AND SYLVIE

Edinburgh, 2011

Ava, Josie, and Catherine had collapsed on the floor of the shed, alone with their own thoughts but in each other's arms. Catherine was the first to break the silence. "Why didn't you tell us, Mum?"

Right then, Ava felt alone, living through the moment she'd always dreamt and hoped for—her twins, reunited and aware of who they were—and yet terrified.

"I wanted to. We—Sylvie and I both wanted to, and we were going to, I promise."

"I don't believe you."

The hurt in Catherine's eyes took Ava's strength away, and she let her head fall back against the wall. As she stared at the dilapidated roof, guilt wrecking through her, she realised Josie was listening without Sylvie there for her.

"We need to get back to your mum, Josie. This isn't fair. She needs to be here, too."

#

Sylvie was trying to distract herself by puttering around Ava's kitchen, telling herself she was just looking for tea bags. Every few minutes she looked at her phone, though, wishing that someone would tell her what was going on.

The simplicity of Ava's home felt comforting. It was smaller, but warmer and less intimidating than her own, with an element of chaos to add to it. Where her house had complete Wedgewood dinner sets and John Lewis glasses arranged in her cupboards, Ava's ones offered mismatched mugs and plastic plates stacked between ceramic plates chipped at the edge.

While pouring water into a mug with '*My house My Rules*' written on the side, Sylvie felt a shiver run through her. She'd caught an odd movement outside the French doors before; hot water spilled on her hand and she squealed, but she kept still. She was so used to being watched that her body acted on autopilot.

You're going mad, Sylvie. He doesn't know where you are.

Michael had been in his home office when she left, and she had taken care to frame her escape as an errand trip. Ava's address was a secret, as she never told him about it or wrote it down.

Except, of course, he would find out. He always did. He would know where she had gone because he had people hack into accounts to read emails and text messages. Michael loved to remind her of this, and she turned a blind eye to it. It was child's play for a man like him.

A new message popped up on her phone, making her jump out of her skin.

We've found her. We are coming home soon. We are all safe, but they know.

She read the words, one at a time, then she read them again. They found Catherine, and she must be okay or Ava would have said. Sylvie's relief was powerful but fleeting.

They know.

Her head spun; perhaps it meant something else. Something painless. Ava wouldn't have told them the truth without Sylvie being there.

The front door swung open.

"Who's there?"

Sylvie told herself it must be Ava's husband coming home, but it was not Sean who met her halfway, however. It was him. He found her.

"Hi, Sylvie. Thought you could just disappear on me, right? How very disappointing."

"Michael, leave me alone. This is not your home."

"Hm, well, it's not your home either, but that didn't stop you from landing here. With a very large bag, I see. Planning on staying a while?"

Now she couldn't speak or move anymore. His eyes told her he would not calm down or be reasonable; real wrath was behind them. *Please, Ava, don't come home with the girls yet,* she prayed. *Let him do what he wants with me and leave before you get here.*

"Thought you pulled off a neat little trick, dredging up those old tarts to spill their dirt on me?"

"I don't know what you mean, Michael."

"Oh, come on now, my dear. How many times have I told you? I'm the brains of this partnership. Don't underestimate me."

"Michael, you need to leave now or I'll call the police."

"Ah, everyone seems to want to do that and I just don't get it."

"You manipulate people. You hurt everyone. I won't let you hurt our daughter again."

"Well, I'm here now, so I may have my own ideas, don't you think?"

Sylvie looked over his shoulder to see if the key was still inside the front door, but that didn't go unnoticed.

"Looking for this?"

He dangled the keyring from his fingers, comic villain style, and she felt her blood run cold.

"The problem is that I'm just that bit faster and stronger than you. You should have lost that weight like I told you to."

"You are every inch the bastard, aren't you?"

"Well, you see. You have got me all cross when I had everything sorted the way I wanted   . You and Josie were very well provided for; all was settled in the world. But you had to go and rock the boat, getting mixed up with that unhinged, child-abandoning friend of yours, and it's been all downhill from there."

By now, his face was mere inches from hers, and spit hit her cheeks as he spoke. "I thought we had an agreement, Sylvie."

"What do you want from me, Michael?"

His tone shifted to lightness, and she knew the worst was still to come.

"Well, it's quite simple," he said. "I need you to come with me now. Come home with Josie, wherever the hell she is, and do your very best job of presenting yourself as the devoted wife who will publicly defend her husband's integrity."

"Like hell I will."

"Oh, dear, that's disappointing. It leaves me with no option than removing you from the picture."

"You wouldn't dare, Michael. How do you reckon you'll get away with that?"

"I have proof of your first attempt on your life, your ongoing mental health issues, and your weakness for prescription medications. It would be easy and believable for you to take your own life now — properly. Maybe using a blunter instrument, a few sharp cuts to the wrist. Might take longer than I would like and get messy, but there would be no margin for mistakes."

"Josie would never believe this. She's old enough to see through you, more than you give her credit for. She'd work it out."

"That's where I disagree. I can be persuasive, you see. Once I explained her how you attempted it before and shown her *your* suicide note, in *your* handwriting, well. I'd say it would be a compelling case."

"You're a monster. You are not human."

"Ah, now, no need for hysterics, Sylvie. I'm pretty sure I gave you plenty of warning," he said. "So, fancy reconsidering the decision to head home and do your duty to sort this mess out?"

Sylvie knew she should feel defeated, but a new strength inside her told her that this man would not control her anymore. She had to think fast.

"Josie's upstairs. Let me go and get her, please."

"Do it quickly. I'm guessing your housemates will be back soon."

Yes, someone would come home soon, but probably not soon enough, and she knew better than underestimating him. He'd follow through with his threats.

"Michael, please, let me get my own coat and bag from the kitchen before I wake her up."

By some twist of luck, Michael's paranoia kept him where he was, standing next to the front window and watching out for any arrivals. "Give me your phone first."

She complied and went to the kitchen, willing her brain to battle through the fear and work on a solution.

The French doors.

Sylvie did not know this house the way she knew her own, which floorboards creaked and would give her away. The French doors looked modern, though, and were unlikely to make too much noise. It was worth the risk, even if she didn't have a penny or a phone to call for help once she was out. She started opening cupboards at random, pretending to look for her coat and hoping this would disguise the noise of her making her final move. Checking once more to ensure she was still alone in the kitchen, Sylvie turned the key as gently as she could.

Silence.

The handle went down and again, it didn't make any noise. She would have heard it above her own rapid breathing, she believed.

Then she was out, into the darkness of the garden where freedom and safety were in touching distance. Sylvie stopped thinking and ran, ran as fast as she could around the side of the house until she reached the side gate. The victory of her escape was sweet, even more so because Josie would be kept safe until they were reunited — Ava would see to that. Michael didn't care about keeping Josie to himself, after all, not as much as trapping Sylvie. Josie was collateral he tolerated to lord over his wife.

 But, just as Sylvie knew her husband too well, she knew he would never let her have the upper hand. And he was waiting. He was waiting for her as she began to taste freedom.   His arm snaked around her waist while he covered her mouth with his hand.

"You really are a stupid bitch, aren't you? Thought you could get one over on me that easily? When will you learn?" he whispered into her ear. "You have chosen not to cooperate, which gives me no choice. You are too damn stubborn to come home, so we are going with plan B — the tragic suicide."

Michael dragged Sylvie through the back door as she sobbed, picturing Josie reading the note after she was gone. He tied her hands and legs with a curtain cord before raiding her handbag; if the look on his face was of any indication, he wanted her to be sedated.

"Hurray! Found them at last. You are depressingly predictable, Sylvie."

"How the hell are you planning to force them down my throat and keep them there, you animal?"

"Don't you worry about the details. You were never the sharpest tool in the box."

She started screaming through the pain of his arm around her neck, she soon gave way to his strength. She stopped screaming, stopped fighting, and just stayed there, on the floor, like   a lamb to the slaughter. She wanted to look him in the eyes, though; she wanted him to see her hatred and horror one more time. Then something else attracted Sylvie's attention. Someone else, standing right outside the door. It was Ava, who held a finger to her mouth. Sylvie felt her husband pull something from his pocket. Her tablets.

"This will all be so much easier when you're asleep now, won't it? Not so much resistance in you then."

Although her fear was still overwhelming, she refused to let it show in her eyes, as she knew   it would make him even stronger. For a split-second, though, Sylvie let her gaze shift behind him. Stopping dead in his tracks, he turned around and saw Ava. Rather, he saw the shine of a number five iron glistening in the air before it connected with his head, Sylvie guessed. Then   his body went weak and slumped in front of her.

Sylvie felt herself close to losing consciousness, but fought back against it as she heard the girls' voices calling for her. The pressure on her chest — Michael had fallen on top of her — eased up and she could speak again.

"Get them out of here, Ava. *Now!*"

"Jesus, Sylvie, what the hell?"

"Get them out and call the police. He was going to — "

"I know. I know, Sylvie. I heard — I heard so much."

Within minutes, the noise of police sirens cut through while blood gathered around Michael's head.

Chapter 39

Ava

Edinburgh 2012

Ava insisted they went to the waterfall on the last Saturday of August. It had to feel the same, smell the same, and the water needed to look as inviting and intimidating as she remembered.

"You go ahead with the girls, Sean. We're wearing flip-flops. Never great on a rocky path."

"You're still wearing those horrific plastic crocodile shoes, Ava."

"Crocs, Sylvie. They're called crocs. And they're bloody comfy and much more practical than those pretentious ankle binders you inflict on yourself."

They were lucky. The sun was out and, considering that over twenty years had passed, the spot was still undiscovered. Just a few dog walkers passing by, or the occasional jogger darting past in lycra and trainers.

"Be careful, girls!"

Although they were twelve going on fifteen, Sylvie still had the tendency to treat Josie like she was a heartbeat away from disaster.

"I'll look after her, Auntie Sylvie," Catherine said. She had already found a spot to lay down their travel rug and lather on the sun cream.

"Other way around, Cat! Follow me – I know the perfect place to hide from this lot!"

Sean stopped close to the water's edge and propped the cooler against the rocks. "Ah, well, mate, guess we can park here and get the beers out."

"Have you been watching Australian soaps on your extended lunch breaks, Sean?"

"Aye, that's just jealousy speaking, Ben. Just 'cause you're stuck in an office all day to pay for Sylvie and Josie's posh shoes."

The women were still a few paces behind them all, taking in every inch of the scene in front of their eyes.

A year after Michael Miller had been charged with attempted murder, he got sentenced to five years in prison. Sylvie knew he would be out again once his time was up, but she wouldn't be alone this time. Ben would be by her side, ready to protect both her and Josie from him.

"They competed against each other today, Sylvie. It was the school debating contest. You should have seen them."

"Do you remember our teenage debates?"

"Yup, and I'm pretty sure I remember winning most of them."
"You always were rather forceful, Ava. One of things I love and hate about you in equal measure."
They watched on as their children sat together on a rock, as close as they could and leaning into each other. Catherine and Josie had secrets to share and the world at their feet.
After taking a deep breath that filled her lungs with the fresh morning air, Ava revelled in a feeling that had crept up on her — she felt free. Freedom had come from understanding that it was okay to need people. And, for the first time since a nosey French girl interrupted her during class, she understood that there were no unpaid debts in a friendship; just more reasons to love each other, truly and deeply.

-the end-

Allison Meldrum has been writing since a very special English teacher with a pocket watch and three-piece suit told her she might be quite good at it. Previously a journalist with a major Scottish newspaper and a national magazine in London, Allison then spent some wild years as a TV Publicist. Returning to her twin loves of Edinburgh and Storytelling, Allison has had multiple short stories published and selected as Editor's Picks by *Toasted Cheese* and *East of The Web* . She has also contributed works to two short story anthologies, *Tolerance* and *Autumn*, through her involvement in Transcendent Authors, a group of international authors who found common inspiration from these themes.

Follow Allison Meldrum at allisonmeldrumauthor.com

Acknowledgements

I would like to thank all of those who contributed to the publication of The Life I Owe Her. Thank you to my wonderful Editor, Christina A. who worked patiently with me to polish my manuscript for publication. Thank you to my cover designer, Sadia Shahid. Thank you to my fellow writers who helped guide me with their expertise and moral support along the way as well as my friends and family who gave me their honest feedback at many stages of the writing process. You know who you are, as they say!

Printed in Great Britain
by Amazon

21323019R00171